THE BRIDE OF A BARONET

LINDA RAE SANDE

Twisted Teacup
PUBLISHING

The Enigma of a Widow

The Secrets of a Viscount

The Widowers of the Aristocracy

The Dream of a Duchess

The Vision of a Viscountess

The Conundrum of a Clerk

The Charity of a Viscount

The Cousins of the Aristocracy

The Promise of a Gentleman

The Pride of a Gentleman

The Holidays of the Aristocracy

The Christmas of a Countess

The Knot of a Knight

The Heirs of the Aristocracy

The Angel of an Astronomer

The Puzzle of a Bastard

The Choice of a Cavalier

The Bargain of a Baroness

The Jewel of an Earl's Heir

The Vixen of a Viscount

The Honor of an Heir

PROLOGUE

April 8, 1840, Wilson Hall, Cockington, Devonshire

Weary and travel sore, Adam Wilson, 5th Baronet of Cockington, stepped down from his dusty coach-and-four in front of his ancestral home and heaved a sigh of relief. Although his shadow loomed before him on the pavers that wound their way between the front gate and the three steps to the portico of the four-story pile known as Wilson Hall, the setting sun hadn't yet disappeared below the horizon. For once, he might be able to say 'good-night' to his daughter before she was asleep.

"Sir Adam," the butler said in surprise when he opened the door to his master's quick knock.

"Harris," Adam acknowledged. "Is Penelope in the

nursery?" he asked as the servant saw to his top hat, greatcoat, and valise.

"She is not, sir. Miss Penelope and Mrs. Longburn are in the parlor. I've left your correspondence and a couple of your daughter's teeth—"

"Mrs. Longburn?" Adam interrupted as he ignored the odd twinge he felt in his chest. "What is *she* doing here?" Another reaction to learning the young widow was in his house was occurring behind the skirt of his top coat, and he was glad he had buttoned it closed when he emerged from the traveling coach.

Harris paused in his duties, as if he had to sort how to best answer the query. "Teaching, sir."

A myriad of possible topics Mrs. Longburn might be engaged in teaching his daughter paraded before his mind's eye, not all of them proper and certainly not appropriate for such a young girl to know. Alarm had his eyes rounding until he remembered she was a parson's widow. Surely she wouldn't be teaching his daughter anything scandalous.

His initial concern was further mitigated when Harris said, "Miss Penelope is learning how to host a dinner party."

Adam blinked again. "She's only six years old."

His own eyes darting to the left, the butler said, "I

believe she is still five, sir, at least until the end of the month."

Adam could feel the heat of embarrassment coloring his neck and face before he passed the servant and marched through the great hall and up the carpeted stairs to the first floor.

Of course his daughter wasn't six. How could he forget her age when it matched the amount of time since his wife had died in the childbed? And why did that sometimes seem like an eternity while other times it felt as if it had happened only yesterday?

About to burst through the closed parlor door, Adam forced himself to pause and take a deep breath. The very last thing he wished to do was frighten Penelope with what he was about to say to Mrs. Longburn. He knew his daughter had taken a liking to the young widow, mostly because she showed her attention that other adults did not.

Aware of voices on the other side, he pressed his ear to the door and listened, grinning when he heard his daughter's voice.

"When we come to the parlor after dinner, how long must we wait until the men join us?" he heard her ask.

"Well, that all depends," Mrs. Longburn replied. "Sometimes one of the gentlemen will note the time and be sure the ladies aren't waiting more than a half-hour. But if they are engaged in a particularly diverting conversation, they may take longer to finish their glasses of port," she explained.

"What's port?"

"It's an after dinner drink for men, darling."

"Can I try it?"

"May...?"

"May I try it?" Penelope asked.

There was a pause before Mrs. Longburn said, "You'll have to ask your father."

Deciding now was the perfect time to make his presence known, Adam knocked once and entered the parlor. Expecting his daughter to come running into his arms, he was startled when the two ladies turned their attentions to him and calmly stood in unison.

At least Penelope *tried* to appear calm. From the way she nearly bounced on the balls of her slippered feet and the half-toothless grin she displayed, Adam knew she was excited to see him.

Mrs. Longburn, not so much. She displayed an expression that might have been guilt or dismay—he couldn't quite tell.

"Ladies," he said as he bowed. "I apologize that I took so long with my port," he said as he approached them, deciding he could pretend he'd come from dinner.

Given the length of time since he'd eaten, he was in truth quite ready for an evening meal.

He lifted first Mrs. Longburn's hand to his lips and then bent down to kiss his daughter's chubby knuckles.

Continuing to bounce in place, Penelope looked as if she was going to launch herself into his arms, but Mrs. Longburn's curtsy had her copying the young widow before she said, "May I pour you a cup of tea, Father?"

Adam gave Mrs. Longburn a nod and then turned back to his daughter, knelt, and pulled her into his arms. "Yes, you may, Poppet," he replied.

"Can." The single word came from Mrs. Longburn, and Adam gave her a brief glance.

"Pardon?"

"Can. Yes, you *can*," she said in a lowered voice.

Adam rolled his eyes. "Yes, my dearest daughter, you *can* pour me a cup of tea," he said as he pulled away from Penelope to regard his only child.

At nearly six, Penelope still displayed the cherubic cheeks of a babe, but her golden blonde hair hung in soft curls to her shoulders. Dressed in a white gown with a white overdress, white stockings, and black slippers, she looked like any other blue-eyed English miss of five who could claim a baronet for a father. What she couldn't claim was a mother, for Alice Winthorpe

Wilson, the love of Adam's life, had died giving birth to her.

"Have you been a good girl?" he asked. "Minded your nursemaid?"

Penelope nodded. "I have," she said shyly. "And Charlotte."

Adam frowned. "Charlotte?"

Mrs. Longburn cleared her throat and Penelope's eyes widened. "Oh, I meant Mrs. Longburn."

Giving the widow a nod, Adam had to resist the urge to say something regarding her Christian name. He had never heard anyone use it since her marriage to the parson, and he wondered how his daughter had come to learn it.

As if Mrs. Longburn could read his mind, she said, "Miss Penelope asked if I had a given name, and I gave her permission to use it when we are in private."

Penelope extracted herself from her father's hold and stood before the tea table. With a quick look at Mrs. Longburn, she lifted the teapot and poured a cup. Not a drop escaped onto the table, but Penelope caught the brief grimace the widow displayed and immediately understood her error. "No," she whined, stomping a foot when she realized her faux pax.

"What is it?" her father asked in alarm.

"I forgot to ask how you take your tea," Penelope replied, her lower lip trembling.

"Why, just like that," he replied, pointing to the cup she had just poured.

Penelope dared a glance at Mrs. Longburn before a watery grin replaced her look of disappointment. "You're doing fine," Mrs. Longburn whispered. "Now what's the next question you ask?" she prompted.

Penelope's eyes rounded. "Would you like cake?" She was once again back to nearly bouncing on the balls of her feet when her father nodded and said, "Oh, yes." About to take a seat, he paused. "Please," he remembered to add, thinking if he didn't do so, he would hear a reminder from the widow.

As Penelope carefully cut a rather large slice of cake, Mrs. Longburn seemed about to put voice to a protest when Adam held out his hand and gave her a quick shake of his head. "I'm starving," he whispered.

Mrs. Longburn nodded her understanding and turned her attention back on her charge.

Penelope attempted to use the serving utensil to place it on a plate when the slice tipped over. Half the cake ended up hanging over the edge, and Penelope looked to the widow. "I've ruined it," she said as she once again stomped a slippered foot.

"You haven't. Simply use the server to push it into

the middle of the plate," Mrs. Longburn instructed, reaching over to place her own hand over Penelope's to guide her. When the cake was somewhat presentable, Penelope held out the plate to her father. Rather than mention the lack of a fork, Mrs. Longburn simply offered him one from across the table, giving him an apologetic look as she did so.

"Thank you, Mrs. Longburn, Miss Penelope," he replied. "Now you must tell me what you've been doing whilst I was in Yorkshire." He patted his knee, and Penelope was quick to move in front of him so he could lift her onto it.

"I'm learning to read," Penelope announced happily.

Adam's gaze immediately went to the widow, but her own eyes were downcast, as if she knew she was caught. "Indeed? Am I to suppose Mrs. Longburn has been your teacher?"

Penelope nodded. "Oh, yes. Every day whilst you were gone, she read to me, and then taught me how to read the words that have two letters," she said with some excitement as she held up two pudgy fingers. "We started the words with three letters today."

"Hmph," Adam responded, hoping his expression wasn't too harsh. Although he appreciated what Mrs. Longburn was attempting to do, he wasn't sure he agreed with the timing. "Are you even old enough to be learning how to read?"

Mrs. Longburn straightened so quickly, Adam was sure a lock of her brilliant red hair might have escaped a pin. He felt a stab of disappointment when he realized it was merely wishful thinking. The widow's coiffure was entirely intact.

For a moment, he imagined plucking every last pin from the perfect bun, flicking it apart with his thumb and forefinger, and combing his fingers through the silken strands. He wondered how long it was. How it would look splayed across his pillow. How it would feel beneath his face after a spirited round of lovemaking.

He had to adjust his daughter's position on his lap lest she notice what else was attempting to take up space there.

"Miss Penelope is nearly six years old," Mrs. Longburn said as she placed her teacup and saucer on the low table.

From the manner in which she sat on the front edge of the settee, Adam thought she looked as if she might bolt from the velvet seat if he said so much as 'boo!' "Is my daughter's education that important to you?" he asked between bites of the cake. Although he hadn't intended to eat such large forkfuls and so quickly, he was hungry.

"It is," the widow replied, wincing when he brought another large bite of cake to his mouth. "I thought you would have seen to a governess for her by now."

It was Adam's turn to wince. He had considered his daughter's education—for about the first five minutes after he had departed Cockington on his latest trip. After that, thoughts of Penelope were pushed aside as he concentrated on the myriad details of what he needed to accomplish during the two weeks he was in York. He would think of her for a few minutes before he fell asleep each succeeding night, the guilt of leaving her behind warring with his need to succeed in his draper business.

"I intended to place an advertisement for the position before I left," he murmured.

"You can't possibly expect to find a suitable governess in the village," Mrs. Longburn countered.

Adam blinked. "I can't?"

Scoffing, Mrs. Longburn furrowed her brows and regarded him as if he'd grown horns on his head. "There isn't a young woman—or an old one, for that matter—who could teach a baronet's daughter what she should know to survive in polite Society," she argued.

Resisting the urge to chuckle at hearing her claim, Adam set his plate on the table and interlaced his fingers as he leaned his elbows on his knees. "Why, I was sure there was at least one," he countered, a brow arching in challenge.

Charlotte Longburn's expression momentarily showed what he thought was fear, and he wondered what she was thinking. Apparently, she really was concerned for his daughter's welfare, but what she expected to receive in return had him curious.

"Who might that be?" she asked in a strangled whisper.

Adam had to once again resist the urge to chuckle at her expense. "Why, you, of course, Mrs. Longburn."

"Me?"

"Yes. You know French, do you not?"

Her eyes darted to the side. "*Oui.*"

"You're already teaching her how to read."

"True."

"You can show Penelope how to draw and paint. How to dance." He waved a hand. "And whatever else it is she needs to know," he added, not really sure what else his young daughter needed to know. Sensing she would argue with him, he continued, "Now, if you'll just give Harris a list of your terms for the employment contract, we can see to an appropriate start date. Day after tomorrow, perhaps?" He stood, lifting Penelope so her bottom rested on a forearm as she wrapped her pudgy arms around his neck. "And in the meantime, Miss Penelope and I are going to have some dinner. Would you care to join us?"

Mrs. Longburn's jaw dropped in a most unladylike manner before she snapped it shut. "Thank you, but... but no. My... my cook is seeing to a meal for me at the parsonage," she stammered.

Adam gave a start. "You're still living *there*?" When he saw how her gaze dropped to the Turkish-carpeted floor and her face took on a blush, Adam felt pity for her. "Do Miss Kate and Miss Eloise still work in the parsonage?" he asked, looking to lighten the mood in the room.

"They do," she affirmed, her gaze lifting to meet his. "Neither apparently has any prospects."

Holding up a finger, Adam shook his head. "Actually, they might," he hedged. "I passed by the Baker boys on my way into town," he said, referring to two of his tenant farmers. The brothers weren't particularly bright, but they were hard workers. They had successfully turned some hardscrabble Wilson ground into a productive farm. "One of them—I can never tell them apart—mentioned he thought this would be the year he would take a wife. He thinks he'll have the winning lamb at this year's village fair, which means he'll earn a fair bit of blunt."

Charlotte gave a start. "You'll be providing the prize money again?"

Adam nodded. "I will. It's a tradition that goes back quite a long time," he replied. "I do wish the fair attracted more people, though. I thought having it on a regular market day would help with attendance, but we never seem to get a good crowd," he lamented. "Apparently it used to be quite the spectacle back in my father's day."

Since she had lived in Cockington for only a few years, Charlotte had attended just three of the village fairs. "Perhaps it needs another contest," she suggested. "Maybe not the pie eating contest, though," she added, wincing at the memory of one of the Baker boys and Elijah Stafford eating berry and lemon pies as fast as they could.

"That was a bit of a mess," Adam agreed. "Although Elijah ended up with a wife out of it," Adam commented with a chuckle. "Even if he didn't like Miss Sherman's lemon pies."

Charlotte's eyes rounded. "He didn't?" she whispered, wondering how he could have consumed four of them during the contest. Then she remembered how he had displayed a rather sour expression after he was declared the winner.

"He hates lemons," Adam said, his attention going

to the parlor window. The sun had nearly set. "Now, about your situation. You say you're still living in the parsonage?" he asked, his gaze turning on the widow. He was sure he saw fear in her expression.

"I am. I... The... the current parson—Mr. Trayfor— he has been most accommodating," she stuttered. "I'm allowed to stay in the cottage until I can find a suitable arrangement. I was thinking of taking a room at Miss Barrow's boarding house." Her head lifted and her chin thrust out in a manner that suggested her momentary discomfort had passed. She was once again the proud widow Longburn.

"Well, there's no need to move into the boarding house," Adam stated. "You can take the apartment on the third floor," he offered. "I rather imagine you living here at Wilson Hall will make it easier to govern... governess... to see to your charge," he said as he once again waved a hand in dismissal.

Mrs. Longburn stared at him. "Move into the home of an unmarried man?" she asked in shock.

Secretly pleased by her response, Adam struggled to keep a straight face. He didn't know why he took such delight in seeing the strait-laced woman so vexed, but he did. That she had been married to Parson Longburn —a man nearly old enough to be her grandfather—

always had Adam wondering what she had seen in the crotchety academic.

He ignored the stab of jealousy he felt at the reminder of her late husband. Tried to erase the memory of seeing her on the arm of the parson as he proudly strutted about the village whilst on their afternoon walks.

Adam dared a glance at his daughter, who apparently understood she was about to gain a governess. The smile on her face once again displayed a distinct lack of two bottom teeth, which had him momentarily curious. "I am a widower, actually," he replied in response to Charlotte's comment. "I'm usually gone more than I'm here in residence, and my apartments are on the second floor. We'll rarely see one another." He paused before he said, "Open your mouth, Poppet."

Penelope dutifully obeyed, and his brows furrowed. "What the...? Whatever has happened to your bottom teeth?"

She beamed in delight. "They fell out when I was eating an apple," she replied, obviously proud.

"Just like that?" he asked, quite unsure as to why she seemed so happy. "Well, where are your teeth now?"

Shrugging, Penelope said, "I don't know. I put them in my shoe."

Adam gave a start. "Your shoe?" he repeated, confusion apparent on his face.

She nodded. "The next day there were two pennies in my shoe," she said as she held up two fingers." I put them in my jewel box," she added in a whisper.

At hearing Mrs. Longburn's throat clearing, Adam lowered Penelope until she was standing on her own. "Go on into the dining room, Poppet," he said, his attention on the widow. "I'll join you in a moment."

Once the girl was beyond the parlor door, he stepped toward the widow. "Did someone send for the physician?" he asked in a hoarse whisper as he took a seat next to her. His eyes blazed in a combination of worry and anger before the floral scent of honeysuckle surrounded him.

Mrs. Longburn's eyes rounded. "Whatever for?"

"My daughter lost her teeth!" He scrubbed his face with a hand, wincing when he realized he was already in need of a shave. "And what's this about pennies in her *shoe*?" he asked as he suddenly stood. He began pacing, his footfalls muffled in the thick Turkish carpeting.

Her eyes widening—she looked as if he thought *she* was the reason the teeth had fallen out—Mrs. Longburn said, "I put them there." When Sir Adam blinked and stopped pacing, she added, "I gave the teeth to Harris and asked that he pass them along to you for safe-keeping."

Adam lifted a fist to his forehead. He used it to rub the space below his dark hair as he groaned.

"Oh!" Mrs. Longburn said with a start, finally understanding the man's point. "It's quite normal for children to lose their small teeth, sir. Their baby teeth. The permanent ones will grow in to replace them. It doesn't take long."

He blinked, vaguely remembering his own two front teeth went missing when he was six years old. He didn't recall finding any blunt in his shoes, however. "And the pennies?"

Mrs. Longburn sighed. "One of the children in the village knew the story about the little mouse. He told her she could trade her teeth for a treat or for money if she left them in her shoe." When Adam continued to stare at her, apparently unfamiliar with the tale, she said, "*La Bonne Petite Souris*," in perfect French.

He rolled his eyes. "Damn French," he muttered. "Pardon my... pardon the curse."

He had almost said, 'French,' but thought better of it.

"Of course, sir. I hope I didn't do wrong, but I didn't want Miss Penelope to be disappointed. The other children all know about the story and have been bragging about the treats they've been receiving when they lose their teeth."

Adam waved a hand as if in dismissal. "It's fine. You did the right thing," he said on a sigh. "I owe you two pennies. I'll add it to your pay." When the faint whiff of his early dinner reached his nose, replacing the light scent of honeysuckle, he added, "May I escort you to the dining room?"

For a moment, the widow looked as if she would accept the invitation, but she shook her head. "No, thank you. It seems I have some work to do. Terms to draw up and such," she added with a wan grin. Not to mention packing, but she still wasn't sure she would accept the offer of the apartment in Wilson Hall. "Besides, given your schedule of late, you really should spend some time alone with Miss Penelope."

Nodding reluctantly, Adam took her hand to his lips and brushed them over the back of her knuckles. "Have a good evening, Mrs. Longburn."

"You as well, Sir Adam," she replied as she dipped a curtsy. "I'll show myself out."

Adam watched as the widow practically ran from the parlor. He might have felt offense at her quick retreat from his presence, but watching her hips sway as she departed more than made up for any perceived cut.

Direct or otherwise.

CHAPTER 1
A WIDOW WITHOUT OPTIONS

few minutes later

Charlotte Wentworth Longburn emerged from Wilson Hall so quickly, she nearly stumbled down the three stairs to the crushed granite drive.

Never had she expected the baronet to offer her employment. Never would she have expected to be offered a paid position with a place to live.

At first, she had thought to turn down Sir Adam's offer outright. How outrageous that he would simply expect her to accept such an offer *and* move into Wilson Hall, no less! But once she was over her initial shock, reason had her reconsidering her reluctance.

A thought of Miss Penelope Wilson had her reconsidering.

The promise Charlotte had made to the girl's

mother, even more so.

She was determined to fulfill that promise, and so far, she had discovered it wasn't a hardship to do so.

As much as she had tried to avoid developing feelings for the tyke, she couldn't help herself. From the moment she had learned of Alice Wilson's death in the childbed, Charlotte had felt sorrow for the newborn babe. Circumstances, such as the baronet's frequent trips away from Cockington, made it possible for her to visit Penelope with the excuse that she looked forward to one day having a babe of her own.

The Wilson Hall nursemaid, Mrs. Heber, was happy for the respite provided when Charlotte spent afternoons with Penelope, so after a time, her more frequent calls were not only appreciated but expected.

Even after she was married to the parson, Charlotte continued to pay calls at Wilson Hall when the baronet wasn't in residence. She delighted in spending time with the young girl, often sitting on the carpeted nursery floor and joining Penelope in her play with dolls or other toys Sir Adam brought back from his trips.

One of Charlotte's hands moved to her middle, and she inhaled softly. Despite her desire to have a child of her own, she had never been blessed with the parson's babe. She knew why, of course, but it only made her want what she couldn't have that much more frustrating.

The dusty coach-and-four in which Adam Wilson had ridden from Yorkshire was still parked in the semi-circular drive, two footmen seeing to a trunk that was mounted on the back and the driver and a groom about to lead the team to the carriage house at the back of the hall.

"Evening, Mrs. Longburn," the driver said as he tipped his hat.

Nodding, Charlotte aimed a tentative smile at John Smithton before her attention went to the west. The sun had already set, and twilight was quickly replacing the brilliant colors that had painted the clouds with peaches and purples only moments earlier. A slight breeze brought the scent of the nearby English Channel. "Good evening, Mr. Smithton, Mr. Coulsden," she replied, including the Wilson Hall groom in her greeting as she dipped a quick curtsy. A look of worry settled over her features. She had stayed entirely too long at Wilson Hall, and it would be dark before she completed the half-mile walk back to the parsonage.

Apparently sensing her unease, John said, "The team is still hitched, Mrs. Longburn. Would you like a ride home? Me wife won't have supper ready for an hour at least."

Charlotte inhaled softly. "It's very kind of you to offer," she replied.

William Coulsden opened the coach door and offered a hand. "It's no trouble, ma'am. Means I can go have supper with the servants and see to the 'orses later."

Charlotte regarded the groom with a knowing look. She knew Mr. Coulsden held a candle for the Wilson Hall housekeeper, Mrs. McNulty, and appreciated any excuse to be in her company.

"If you're sure it's no trouble," she replied. Charlotte stepped up and into the coach. The exterior lamps were both lit, and she inhaled softly upon seeing the light blue velvet squabs and blue curtains that graced the glass windows on either side.

She had assumed the baronet would have leather seats in his traveling coach. The thought of the widower's late wife had her reconsidering. Lady Wilson would have chosen the interior fabrics. Blue had been Alice's favorite color.

Settling in so she sat facing the direction of travel, Charlotte suppressed the urge to audibly sigh with pleasure as the coach jerked into motion.

Surrounded by the scents of citrus and amber, Charlotte closed her eyes and took a deep breath, reminded of how Adam Wilson had smelled for those brief moments he had been sitting next to her in the parlor. Although she had been tempted to complain—he had sat entirely too close to her—she had remained silent.

It wasn't that his cologne was overpowering, for it was quite pleasant. It wasn't that she was frightened by the baronet—she wasn't. But for some reason, Adam Wilson reminded her of what might have been. What might have been if her father, Franklin Wentworth, hadn't insisted she marry his friend, Ambrose Longburn.

I'll see you wed before I die, he had announced upon her twenty-third birthday. Although she hadn't known her father was nearly at death's door, he obviously had, for she was betrothed the following fortnight and married three weeks later.

Apparently her father didn't care that she would be a widow after only a few years. Ambrose Longburn had been about the same age as her father.

Looking back, she now wished her father hadn't taken her comment about living close to Alice's daughter so seriously. Thoughts of having a child of her own had her wishing he had chosen somewhere else for them to live after her own mother had died of cholera.

Back then, they had lived in London whilst her father taught at a local school for boys. By choosing to settle in Cockington, her father had unwittingly limited

Charlotte's options for an advantageous marriage. Other than a few farmers or fishermen who lived at least a mile from the village and the old parson who had traveled with them from London, there weren't any eligible bachelors in search of wives.

Charlotte had known Parson Longburn even before her father had moved them to Cockington. Having sat through his interminably long sermons every Sunday morning, she knew he was a learned man—a scholarly man who reveled in his study of history and philosophy. Having acted as hostess for the frequent dinners when her father hosted the parson, she knew him to be polite and civil and well-respected by all the villagers.

He was also one of the few men who was taller than she was.

If only the parson hadn't thought of her as an empty-headed female.

He rarely spoke to her of more than domestic concerns or tales from his youth. It wasn't until after they were married that she had learned Ambrose had spent his boyhood near Cockington. After he finished his schooling, he had ended up with an Anglican parish in London and lived in the capital until his request to take on the parish in the Cockington area was granted.

Despite the interest she pretended in his scholarly pursuits, Ambrose never shared what he was studying whilst they ate dinner. He answered her occasional queries, choosing his words carefully, as if he thought she couldn't understand his explanations. Whenever they were in the parsonage, he behaved as if she didn't exist. As if she were a mere servant.

But when they walked about the village or in nearby Torquay, Ambrose Longburn proudly escorted her on his arm, his manner almost jovial with those who greeted them. The first time it had happened, Charlotte had thought something was wrong with him. How could he act one way behind closed doors and quite another when in the company of others?

After a few weeks, she noticed how the other men in the village regarded him, waggling their brows and making comments that were clearly meant to be taken in a manner different from how they sounded to her.

Embarrassment colored her cheeks when she realized what the villagers all thought.

If only they knew the truth of the situation.

Well, it mattered not now. Ambrose was dead, and his replacement had arrived in the village only a month later. Michael Trayfor was not only much younger than Ambrose, he was friendlier. His sermons were also shorter and his services better attended than those of his predecessor.

He was also patient, for Charlotte had no place to live

other than the parsonage. Her father's home had been inherited by a distant cousin and sold to a local merchant. The new parson insisted she remain where she was until such time as a different situation presented itself. *I already have the benefit of a place to live*, he had told her, referring to Miss Barrow's boarding house. *And it doesn't cost me anything*, he had added as he waggled his brows.

Charlotte remembered gasping before he explained why it was he was able to live there rent free. When he asked that she keep the news to herself, Charlotte was more than happy to comply. She was friends with Miss Barbara Barrow, after all, and keeping their secret was a source of amusement she experienced every time she heard gossip about the new parson.

Remembering Sir Adam's offer of an apartment, Charlotte realized a different situation had presented itself. Although she could move into the boarding house, making it possible for Michael Trayfor to inhabit the parsonage, she could simply choose to live at Wilson Hall.

Charlotte sighed and once again inhaled, rather enjoying the citrus and amber scents left behind by the baronet. Having spent most of the past fortnight at Wilson Hall with Penelope, Charlotte knew those scents well. They lingered about the study and the parlor, the dining room and the breakfast parlor. Sometimes they were even evident in the nursery.

Ambrose had never smelled of anything but old wool and sour breath.

As the coach took the slight turn into the village, Charlotte's thoughts drifted back to Adam Wilson's offer of employment. His offer of a place to live.

For a moment, she imagined waking up in Wilson Hall instead of the tiny parsonage. Waking up to citrus and amber-scented bed linens. Waking up to discover she wore nothing in the way of a night rail. Waking up to see Adam Wilson gazing down at her, mischief in his eyes.

Before she could imagine what might come next, the coach stuttered to a halt and a moment later, Mr. Smithton opened the door.

"Thank you so much, Mr. Smithton," she said as the driver offered a hand, glad for the dark given how she was sure her cheeks were bright red with what she had just imagined. She stepped down and regarded the dimly lit parsonage.

"Would you like me to escort you to the door, ma'am?" A light rain had begun to fall, and droplets collected on the driver's tricorn hat.

Pulling the key to the front door from her reticule—

she rather doubted either of the servants would hear her knock—Charlotte said, "That won't be necessary."

With a nod to the driver, she made her way into the house and an evening of restless thoughts.

What else could she do but accept the baronet's offer? Where else could she live given her meager monies?

As the rain pattered on the parsonage roof, Charlotte pulled a sheet of parchment from the parson's desk. Dipping the pen into the little bit of ink that remained in the pot, she wrote her response to the baronet's offer.

> *Dear Sir Adam,*
>
> *After careful deliberation, I have decided to accept your offer of employment as governess for your daughter, Miss Penelope, and your offer of an apartment in which to live whilst I perform my duties. In return, I request—*

Here Charlotte stopped writing. What did she want in return for acting as Penelope Wilson's governess? What did governesses earn in pay in similar circumstances?

One pound a month seemed entirely too little. She would be spending the majority of her day seeing to

Miss Penelope. Three pounds seemed almost too much given she would have room and board at Wilson Hall.

Two pounds. Surely Sir Adam could afford two pounds a month. Word in the village suggested he was one of the wealthiest men in Devonshire.

She resumed writing the letter.

Two pounds per month in compensation and Sunday mornings off to attend church services.

Her own servants had all day Sunday to spend as they saw fit, but she knew she would wish to spend them in Miss Penelope's company. She adored the young girl.

I can begin my duties—

Here Charlotte glanced up to discover Kate, the cook, regarding her with a quirked brow and her arms crossed over her substantial bosom. "What is it?" she asked in alarm.

"Your dinner is cold," Kate replied. "Again."

Charlotte managed a look of contrition. "I'll be right there," she replied as she quickly returned her attention to the letter.

On the morrow.

Thank you for the opportunity.

Sincerely yours,

Mrs. Charlotte Longburn

Charlotte set the cork stopper on the ink bottle. Had the servant been able to read, she might have turned the letter over. Instead, she simply dropped the quill and stood. "I've just accepted a position," she stated. "I'll be moving out of this cottage tomorrow." She rather enjoyed how the cook blinked, her mouth dropping open as Charlotte passed her on the way toward the tiny dining room.

"A *position*?" Kate repeated, her brows waggling.

"Really, Kate," Charlotte protested as she turned to regard the cook with a look of rebuke. "Must you think the worst of me always?"

The cook rolled her eyes. "You are rather easy to tease," she replied with a shrug. She crossed her arms and leaned against the door jamb. "I would have guessed seamstress for Madame de la Quois, but I know you can't sew a straight stitch—"

"Kate!" Charlotte protested. Madame de la Quois was the only woman in nearby Torquay who could claim to be a modiste.

"—Or a maid in someone's household, but you

haven't the experience. Which means..." She frowned. "Mistress for Mr. Barkers at the mercantile in Torquay?"

"Kate!" This time Charlotte moved her hands to her hips and glared at the servant. How could anyone think she would do such a thing as prostitute herself? She had been raised as a gentleman's daughter. Been a parson's wife. And for the past year, she'd been a perfectly respectable widow.

The cook merely rolled her eyes, as if she didn't care she had offended her mistress. "Does it really matter, Lottie? It's not like you can behave like most widows," she replied, making a suggestive move with her hips. "Everyone in Cockington would know."

"And all the wives would shun you," Eloise, the housekeeper, said as she stepped up to join Kate.

For a moment, Charlotte realized that in all of Cockington, the three of them were the only unattached women of marriageable age. Given the number of younger bachelors, she wondered how it was these two women were still unmarried. Neither were educated, but they were handsome enough with their dark blonde hair and blue eyes.

"I've no intention of becoming anyone's mistress," Charlotte stated. "I have, however, accepted the position of governess for Miss Penelope Wilson."

The two servant's stared at her a moment before they broke out in laughter.

"Governess?" Kate repeated, her amusement slowly fading from her face.

"Sir Adam's daughter?" Eloise asked in a whisper.

Rather happy to see she had the servants startled into near silence, Charlotte said, "I start my employment the day after tomorrow, but I plan to move into Wilson Hall on the morrow. That way, Reverend Trayfor can move in here before he gives his next sermon."

The two servants quickly sobered and exchanged glances. "You don't think he'll wish to stay on at the boarding house?" Eloise asked.

Charlotte furrowed a brow, tempted to share what she knew. Instead, she feigned ignorance. "Why would he? He has to pay Miss Barrows to live there, does he not?"

Glancing at one another again, the two servants both broke out in a fit of giggles. They obviously believed the new parson wasn't as pious as he seemed.

Not about to set them straight, Charlotte huffed and made her way to the dining room to eat her dinner.

She didn't even mind that the food was cold.

CHAPTER 2
LEAVING AN OLD LIFE

he following day

Despite the light rain that had continued to fall since the evening prior, Charlotte was determined to have all her belongings packed and moved into Wilson Hall before that evening's supper.

She had already been to Wilson Hall once that morning. Ensconced beneath the hood of her late husband's prized curricle as well as a blanket, she had taken the reins of the black Friesian and managed to make the short trip to Wilson Hall without so much as a drop of water landing on her person.

Her large umbrella had helped in that regard.

The return trip was another matter entirely. She entered the parsonage soaked to the skin, only her coiffure having survived the blinding rain due to the large hat she had donned for the trip.

Upon her arrival at Wilson Hall, she hadn't expected to hand her letter of acceptance to the baronet personally. She had thought to merely give it to Harris and ask that it be passed on. But Sir Adam had emerged from his study upon hearing her arrival and joined the butler in the vestibule.

"Two pounds?" he had questioned, after perusing her written words.

Charlotte remembered doubting her decision to request that particular amount, but she held her ground. "Yes, sir. I believe that is the appropriate pay for a governess."

"Hmph," he had replied with a shrug. "Very well. Mrs. McNulty can show you to your apartment."

Then the infuriating man had simply turned around and disappeared into his study.

Well, she was a servant now, she supposed.

Sort of.

She wouldn't be taking her meals with the staff, and probably not with Sir Adam, either, unless he wanted Miss Penelope at his table.

Well, she hadn't exactly been dining with others this past year at the parsonage. Her new life as a governess would be much the same as it had been as a parson's widow, except now she would be spared the struggle of traveling to and from Wilson Hall on the days she wanted to be with Penelope.

After a quick tour of her sitting room, bedchamber, and bathing chamber—all rather more elegant than she had expected to find in the Georgian-era Wilson Hall— Charlotte had rushed back to the parsonage to collect her things and begin the process of moving. Mr. Smithton would arrive in a few hours with the baronet's coach and the groom, Mr. Coulsden. They had both insisted on helping her with the move, and she had gladly accepted their offer.

In her haste to return to the parsonage, Charlotte neglected to cover her gown with the blanket. The wind-driven rain had blown directly into the curricle, soaking her and the interior of the equipage.

"It's not the least bit funny," she said when Eloise met her at the front door of the parsonage, doing a poor job of suppressing a grin at seeing her mistress in a state of dishabille.

"I canna' believe you intend to move *today* of all days," the maid said as she handed Charlotte a linen towel.

"I do and I will," Charlotte replied as she did her

best to dry the front of her gown. Determined to be ready when the Wilson Hall driver and groom arrived to collect her, Charlotte set about packing her two trunks and a valise. Two tours of every room in the parsonage but those of the servants had her deciding she had everything that belonged to her.

She stared into the trunks. Her entire life's possessions and clothes barely filled the wooden containers.

Seven-and-twenty years' worth.

Kneeling next to the trunk containing her trousseau, she fingered the muslin of a snowy white night rail and then the pastel threads of an elaborate embroidery on a pillow covering, the white Bavarian lace on the neckline of her come-out gown, and the delicate silk of her favorite shawl. Beneath those were various gowns and petticoats, corsets and slippers.

In the other trunk, she found the doll she had played with from the time she could walk. Her mother, Caroline Wentworth, had still been alive back then. The woman's jewel box rested at the bottom of the trunk, its meager contents including only her wedding ring and a parure of pearls her father had bestowed on her over the course of their marriage—a bracelet, necklace, pendant, earbobs, and a brooch.

Charlotte opened the box, relieved to find the jewels were all still in their place. Against the black velvet lining, the pearls shimmered in the dim candlelight.

Plucking the earbobs from the box, Charlotte was examining them when Eloise found her. "The Wilson coach is here for you," she said.

"Oh," Charlotte replied in surprise as she closed the trunks and then lifted herself from the floor. Where had the time gone? Still clutching the earbobs in one hand, she realized she had best put them on or risk losing them. "I'm sure the parson will be in touch soon," she said as she made her way to the kitchen. "I'm off, Kate. I'll no doubt see you at church," she said, deciding a formal farewell wasn't necessary. Remembering Sir Adam's comment from the day before, she paused and said, "Oh, and if you haven't heard, apparently one of the Baker boys is looking to marry this year. Not sure which one, though."

Kate's mouth dropped open in shock. "I won't be believing it until there's a ring on my finger," she replied as she held up a hand. "'Asides, they don't have an extra penny betwixt 'em," she groused.

Donning her redingote and hat, Charlotte said her farewells to Kate and Eloise before she opened the door.

"What about the curricle? And the horse?" Kate asked.

"I spoke with Reverend Trayfor. They belong to him now," Charlotte replied, remembering how surprised Barbara had been when she'd told the two at the boarding house about her decision. It wasn't as if she could afford to keep a horse.

Charlotte made her way to the coach. The driver and the groom had already loaded her trunks onto the back of it. Seated with her valise next to her, she watched through the rain-streaked window as the coach pulled away.

For once in her life, Charlotte was glad to leave her home. As for her new one, she had an idea and was looking forward to setting it into motion. She just hoped her new employer would agree. Although she had no intention of upending his life in Wilson Hall, he was about to discover his young girl had outgrown the nursery.

an hour later

Recalling that moment in the coach as she stood with her hands on her hips, Charlotte regarded the fourth story of Wilson Hall with a grin of satisfaction.

The former ballroom, now a repository for old furnishings and boxes filled with whatnot, included a large fireplace as well as a multi-level stage where orchestras had played in the past. Windows along both long walls meant there was plenty of light. There was the main entrance at one end of the room, and another from the servants' stairs at the other end.

She could certainly imagine the room filled with ball-goers dressed in their finest. Hear the five-piece chamber orchestra playing a Scotch reel and the waltz.

Now it would make a perfect playroom.

"What do you think?" she asked as she glanced down at Penelope. The youngster was mimicking Charlotte, her hands on her hips. "Do you suppose this could be your playroom?"

Penelope's eyes rounded as she looked up at her new governess. "Indeed. And you can teach me here, too," she remarked.

As Charlotte considered the room's size, she realized Penelope had a good point. There was plenty of space to set up a classroom. The more she considered the idea, the better she liked it.

Once the large space was emptied, she could have some of the items from the nursery brought up. A table and the two small chairs. The book case. Mayhap some of the discarded furnishings could be put to use to make a parlor.

Charlotte inhaled softly at the thought that Alice

would have agreed with her plan to make a playroom for her daughter. She would have agreed with her efforts to educate the young girl in becoming a young lady. Penelope seemed willing and able.

Charlotte could only hope the girl's father wouldn't object to their plan.

CHAPTER 3
A CURIOSITY FROM THE ATTIC

he following day, the Wilson Hall study

When the dusty box landed on Sir Adam's mahogany desk, he winced and gave the footman a quelling glance. "Please tell me this is the last one," he said as he gingerly lifted the lid off the carton.

"'Tis, sir. And all the old furnishings have been removed as well."

Sir Adam gave the servant a look of worry. "To where?" Outside, rain continued to fall as it had for the past two days. If all the objects had been removed from Wilson Hall's attic and put somewhere outside, he could only imagine how soaked they would be.

At least they would no longer be dusty. From the

layer of dirt atop the boxes that rested on his desk, though, he imagined a muddy mess.

"Mrs. Turner fussed a bit, but she let us use the room where she does the laundry. There's not much, really. Things are stacked willy nilly, but… until you decide what you'd like done with the stuff, it's not in her way." He angled his head. "Not all of the furnishings came down," he added. "Apparently Mrs. Longburn has plans for some of it up there."

His master rolled his eyes. "I cannot believe I allowed her to talk me into this," Adam said in dismay. The woman had only been in residence for slightly more than a day, and she had already upended his quiet life in the country. If it hadn't been for Penelope's excitement over the project, he might not have agreed.

The footman shrugged. "It's quite an impressive space, sir. Mrs. McNulty claims it used to be a ballroom." The hall's housekeeper, Mrs. McNulty had been employed far longer than any other servant on the estate.

Adam looked up from the box he had opened. "The attic?" he countered in disbelief. All he could remember from his brief forays into the top story of the country estate house was a collection of his grandfather's oddities and the three boxes that now took up half of his study's desktop.

"Indeed. Mrs. McNulty has the upstairs maids sweeping it out right now," he explained.

Rain continued to pelt the study's two windows, reminding Adam why he had agreed to Charlotte Longburn's suggestion—insistence, was more like it—that the attic be reconfigured to create a playroom and a classroom for Penelope.

"She's outgrown the nursery, Sir Adam," Charlotte had explained the day before, after her second arrival.

Her first arrival had her delivering a letter accepting the offer to be Penelope's governess and the terms under which she would work for him.

Charlotte's demand of two pounds per month in compensation had surprised him. Adam had expected she would ask for four pounds and then accept three when he countered her proposal. Two pounds per month seemed a bargain, at least until he was faced with the new reality of another servant in his household. One who wasn't shy about suggesting changes.

"And the old ballroom would make for a perfect place for her to play on days when it's raining. Like today," he recalled her saying in defense of her decision to upend his life.

How Charlotte had managed to arrive in the middle of a blinding rainstorm without so much as a hint of water on her person had Adam curious. Although he hadn't seen her umbrella, he imagined it was wider in diameter than she was tall.

And she was tall.

Nearly as tall as him, and given the ridiculous hats she wore—wide-brimmed creations adorned with all manner of ribbons and silk flowers—her arrival anywhere could not be ignored.

Even when she'd been forced to wear widow's weeds the year prior, her black hats could be seen long before her gorgeous red hair was apparent.

He often wondered if her late husband appreciated her red hair. As the parson for Cockington for only three years, Ambrose Longburn had delivered long sermons on Sundays and graveside eulogies at the few funerals that took place in the small cemetery at the edge of the village. Although he was respected, he was not a likable fellow. He bragged about his scholarly pursuits and would argue philosophy with anyone who dared counter his point of view. Worse, though, was how he would proudly squire his wife about the village as if he owned it, showing off Charlotte as if she were some sort of prize he'd won at the local fair.

Adam shook off the unpleasant memories of Parson Longburn, only to be reminded of his own situation.

Having spent his first two years as a widower in London—Adam's late wife's family had insisted he and his newborn daughter live with them in their townhouse in Cavendish Square—Adam had returned to Cockington shortly before Charlotte's arrival in the village. He wasn't even aware she had moved to Cockington when she did, accompanied by her father and the Parson Longburn. At least, not until he learned Charlotte Wentworth had married the village parson by way of the *Torquay Chronicle*. If he hadn't known anything about his wife's best friend, he would have assumed Charlotte Wentworth was really the parson's daughter, their ages were so disparate.

He had almost felt sorry for Charlotte, and he had certainly envied the parson.

"He was a very learned man, Sir Adam," she had explained when he finally asked how it was she came to marry the parson. "Besides the Baker brothers, there weren't any other unmarried men available when my father, may he rest in peace, decided it was time I enter into matrimony."

Adam remembered wincing at hearing her options. The Baker brothers were both tenant farmers, but neither struck him as being particularly bright. He doubted either one of them could even read.

She would have appreciated their hard work, though. They never seemed to complain, and he supposed the credit for that went to their mother. The matron was one of the organizers for the annual village fair. Mrs. Mildred Baker could be considered a busybody, but she was also good for Cockington. He was fairly sure she could read, so he reconsidered his opinion of the grown boys. Perhaps they could read.

Charlotte could certainly read. Part of the time she spent with Penelope involved teaching her how to read. The rest of the time, the two would have their attentions on an open book whilst Charlotte read aloud in a most expressive voice. Or voices, rather, for she would change the pitch and delivery of her words for each character, delighting his daughter as she practically performed the stories.

The memory of discovering his daughter sitting on Charlotte's lap while the two sat in the nursery's wooden rocking chair came to mind, and he inhaled softly. Charlotte had been reading whilst Penelope stared at her profile, apparently engrossed by the way she performed the fairytale.

Obviously not one of the scary ones written by the Grimm brothers.

Charlotte's ever present hat was nowhere to be found. Her red hair had been styled in a riot of curls and ringlets, a style so similar to the way his late wife had worn her hair, he thought Alice Winthorpe had come back to life. Adding to the dreamlike quality of the moment, the summer light from the nearby window had cast the her and his daughter in an ethereal glow occasionally interrupted by a cascade of dust motes as the pages of the book were turned.

The reminder of dust had Adam giving his head a shake.

"Are you all right, sir?"

Adam jerked his head up to discover the footman, Connors, still stood on the other side of his desk. "A little lost in thought is all. Tell me, what sorts of furnishings did you find in the attic?"

The servant's chin briefly doubled as he considered the query. "A couple of small tables. Some chairs. A settee. Most everything is, uh, *feminine* you could say."

This bit of information had Adam's brow arching. "Oh? Anything broken... or in need of repair?"

Connors seemed to think on the query a moment. "No, sir. It's all in good shape, although the settee could probably use some new upholstery."

"Hmph."

As if he could read the baronet's mind, the footman leaned over the desk and said, "Sir Winston didn't want any reminders of his wife after she died, sir. Loved her dearly, he did, but the furniture had to go."

Suspicion had Adam scoffing. "How is it you know

such a thing? You don't appear old enough to have served my grandfather."

"No, sir," Connors concurred. "But my father did. According to him, Winston Wilson might have been the third baronet of Cockington, but there almost wasn't a fourth."

Adam furrowed a brow. "Whatever do you mean?"

Connors leaned in closer. "Seems your grandfather couldn't decide who to take to wife." Before he could say more, the sound of a clearing throat had Adam and Connors turning to discover Harris, the rather portly butler, standing on the study's threshold.

"Pardon me, sir," Connors whispered as he stepped back from the desk and gave a short bow. He quickly took his leave of the study.

Before Adam could react, Harris rolled his eyes and took one step into the study. "I wish to apologize, sir. Connors won't bother you again."

Disappointed the footman hadn't been able to complete his story, Adam allowed a shrug. "He wasn't. Not really," he replied. "But now that *you're* here, perhaps you can enlighten me as to why my grandfather wanted all the reminders of my grandmother removed to the attic."

Harris' eyes rounded. "I cannot say, sir. I wasn't aware there was a reason other than that the furniture was… was superfluous, sir." He motioned to the boxes on the desk and added, "Perhaps you'll find the answer in one of those containers. The one on top has 'family records' written on the side."

Adam's attention went to the top box and he sighed. Although he had planned to ride his horse to Torquay for a late luncheon, the incessant rain meant his time would be better spent rifling through old papers. "Bring tea," he ordered as he removed the lid from one of the boxes. "Looks as if I'll be spending the afternoon brushing up on my family history."

"Very good, sir."

Remembering the comment about the furniture from the attic, Adam said, "Have Mrs. McNulty see to the reupholstery of the furniture that's been brought down. There are some bolts of velvet down in the storeroom Mr. MacGyver can use," he added, referring to the village upholsterer. "Couldn't sell them at the shop in London, so he may as well make use of them on the furniture." When he noted Harris' look of confusion, he added, "I'd like it made ready for my daughter's new playroom."

The butler nodded, although his look of confusion remained in place. "Very good, sir," Harris replied before he disappeared.

Settling back into his leather chair with a stack of

papers, Adam had barely finished reading the second page when he straightened. He held up the third sheet of parchment, an advertisement for the village fair. Although the printing was faded, he could easily make out the announcement as well as the curious addendum near the bottom.

The Lady Wilson Contest

Winston Wilson, 3rd Baronet of Cockington, will choose his wife from those eligible young ladies entered into a contest to become Lady Wilson. Girls must be of marriageable age and free of scandal. No widows, please. Enter at the special booth at the fair!

Adam re-read the announcement several times before he guffawed. Pawing through the next few sheets of paper, he discovered a list of about twenty ladies' names followed by words like "sings,""plays piano," "sews," and "paints." He reviewed the names, finally finding the listing for his grandmother.

Gertrude Amherst, 22, plays piano and sings.

He let out a snort and rolled his eyes.

However could his grandfather choose a wife from contestants at a village fair?

A silver tea tray appeared, and Adam looked up to discover Mrs. McNulty beaming in delight. "Afternoon, sir," she said. "Such an improvement up in the ballroom. Why, Miss Penelope will have the perfect place in which to play house. I've already dispatched a note to Mr. MacGyver to see to reupholstering the settee."

Realizing his desk had no room for the tray, Adam quickly moved one of the cartons to the floor. "Very good," he acknowledged as she set the tray onto the desk and then went about pouring him a cup of tea. "I'm sure she'll enjoy the ballroom when it's suitably outfitted, but as for playing house, I cannot help but wonder why she doesn't just use this one?" he commented as one of his hands waved to indicate Wilson Hall. "She would practically have the run of it if she wanted," he added.

Mrs. McNulty lifted a gnarled hand. "Oh, young ladies want their own house, of course," the housekeeper replied. "A place to keep their doll. Hold their own tea parties. Host a friend or… or their father," she hinted.

Adam scoffed. "She's never invited me for tea," he murmured. "I hear Mrs. Longburn frequently has that honor, though," he added, failing to keep the sound of jealousy from his voice. One of the times Charlotte Longburn had been to Wilson Hall, she and Penelope had enjoyed an afternoon tea in the orangery. Both dressed in spring frocks and flowered hats, the two had walked hand-in-hand to the brick and glass building on the west side of the property, no doubt engaged in whatever conversation a young girl could have with a young widow.

He wouldn't have given them a second glance except he couldn't help but notice the gentle sway of Charlotte's skirts as she walked. Given her height, he could only imagine the length of the limbs beneath those skirts. Imagine the curve of her calves, the bend of her knees, the long thighs and how they might feel wrapped around his. Imagine the hips at the top of those thighs. The globes of her shapely bottom.

"Perhaps Miss Penelope is waiting to be invited to tea with *you*," Mrs. McNulty suggested, her eyes darting to the tea tray. She had included an extra cup and saucer on the salver as well as an extra slice of cake.

Blinking away the thought of Charlotte Longburn's shapely bottom, Adam furrowed his dark brows. "Has Mrs. Longburn ever invited her to tea?"

"Indeed, sir. Miss Penelope joined her at the parsonage every Friday afternoon," the housekeeper replied, her expression making it apparent she was surprised he wasn't aware. "Oh, dear. I thought you knew, sir."

Deciding he would look the fool if he asked how long the arrangement had been going on, Adam pointed to the tea tray. "Cook was awfully generous with the sweets today," he said with an appreciative grin.

"Cook included an extra slice of cake, seeing as how it's raining," she said as she offered him his cup and saucer.

Not sure why the one meant the need for the other, Adam decided not to ask. Despite having had breakfast, he was starving.

"Or you could just share it with a guest," Mrs. McNulty hinted with an arched brow. She curtsied and hurried from the study, as if she feared a scolding.

Adam sighed and regarded the extra cake and cup and saucer for a moment before he called out, "Harris."

The butler appeared a moment later. "Sir?"

"Is my daughter in residence?" He managed to keep a wince from showing. If Penelope wasn't in residence, she would be drowning in the downpour still occurring outside.

Harris' eyes rounded. "Why, I believe she's in the nursery, sir."

"Good. Have her nursemaid bring her here," Adam

ordered. "I'd like her to join me for tea." Remembering how petite Penelope was, and the comment Connors had made about the tables from the attic being feminine, he added, "And have Connors bring a small table and chair for her to use."

"Yes, sir." Looking as if he might faint, Harris gave a slight bow and backed out of the study.

Adam resisted the urge to chuckle at the butler's expense and turned his attention back to the papers from the box.

CHAPTER 4
SERVANTS REVEAL SOME SECRETS

*M*eanwhile, in the kitchen

"Why, you look as if you're the cat who's swallowed a canary," William Coulsden said as Mrs. Margaret McNulty hurried into the kitchen. He had been perched on the bench at the trestle, a cup of coffee in one hand and a plate of sliced meats and cheese set before him, but he had stood upon her arrival, his chest thrust out as attempted to suck in his growing belly.

Mrs. McNulty gave the groom a slight curtsy. "Don't you know it," she replied as she made her way to the stove where the teakettle was steaming. "Just came from the baronet's office. It seems Mrs. Long-burn's suggestions have him a bit bothered," she happily claimed.

Grinning at the housekeeper's delight, William returned to his seat. "You're referring to the old ballroom?"

The housekeeper inhaled softly. "Indeed," she said, indicating her surprise that he knew it wasn't merely an attic.

"I remember the last ball Sir Winston hosted up there," he claimed.

Having finished pouring a cup of tea, Mrs. McNulty whirled around and stared at the groom. "What's this you're saying?"

"Seemed like everyone from Torquay, Livermead, and Cockington was in attendance," William went on, as if he hadn't heard her question. "All those beautiful gowns. Men all dressed up in their Sunday clothes. Why, you would have thought it was a right proper ball in London."

Mrs. McNulty regarded him with a curious expression. "Were you even old enough to *be* there?" she asked, suspicion evident in her voice.

Happy for the opportunity to spend some time with the housekeeper, William waved her to the trestle. "I was about four or five," he admitted. "Came in from the stables. Hid out at the top of the servants' stairs. And I wasn't the only one spyin' on the ball," he said in a whisper. "I think there were four or five of us up there watchin' the festivities."

Taking the seat across from him, the housekeeper asked, "How *did* you come to be the stable boy here?"

William straightened and pushed his plate in her direction. "Help yourself. There's more here than I'll eat," he offered, thrilled that the housekeeper was willing to spend some time with him. He had secretly held a candle for the housekeeper for some time, but he was far too shy to do anything about it. "Got hired because, well, most of the family worked here after Sir Winston married my great aunt, Gertrude."

Mrs. McNulty's mouth dropped open. "No," she replied in disbelief.

"It's true. She hired me mother as her lady's maid. Me in the stable, me father as the baronet's secretary. Her marrying Sir Winston meant our family didn't have ta leave Cockington to find work."

Her brows furrowed slightly. "But if your great aunt married a Wilson..." She paused to consider his relationship with the current baronet. "That makes you a cousin of some sort to Sir Adam, does it not?."

William chuckled. "It does indeed. A second one, I think, but I don't mind," he said proudly. "Neither does my brother."

"That would be Mr. Coulsden? At the mercantile?"

"Theodore, yes, ma'am," he affirmed. "He's my older brother."

"Hmm," she murmured before she took a sip of tea. "Have you ever thought to work anywhere else? Other than Wilson Hall?"

William tugged on his earlobe. "Can't say as I have," he replied. "Always liked it here. Good horses. Been promoted to groom, and I'll be the driver when Mr. Smithton retires. Probably next year."

This bit of news seemed to interest the housekeeper. "Oh, will you now?"

His face displayed a reddish cast at hearing her response. "I know being a groom isn't exactly the best position for a man of my age, but I do hope you don't hold it against me, Mrs. McNulty."

She shook her head. "I wouldn't do that, Mr. Coulsden."

William seemed about to say something else when Mr. Smithton entered the kitchen. "There you are," he said when he spotted the groom. He tipped his hat in the housekeeper's direction. "Mrs. McNulty."

"Oh, I was just eatin' my luncheon," William said, obviously annoyed he hadn't had a chance to continue his conversation with the housekeeper.

"Well, when you're done, I could use some help with moving the coach. About time we built that new stall," Mr. Smithton said. "Given this rain, I doubt we'll be doing anything out of doors for a day or two."

"Of course," William replied, hurrying to gather up the cheese. He turned his attention on the housekeeper. "One of the mares is expecting," he said by way of explanation. "Gotta make room for a foal in the stable."

Mrs. McNulty nodded her understanding. "Seems as if Wilson Hall is growing more crowded this year."

Mr. Smithton chuckled. "Wait until the baronet decides to remarry," he commented.

William glanced up at the driver. "What makes you say that?"

Shrugging, the driver said, "He needs an heir. That means there will be a new Lady Wilson, and then there will be more little ones runnin' about the house," he added as his hand waved about at this side.

Tittering, Mrs. McNulty finished her tea and stood, which had William doing the same. "We have to get him married off first," she said with a grin.

William watched her leave the kitchen before he heaved a sigh. "Your timing is terrible, Smitty," he murmured.

Rolling his eyes, Mr. Smithton scoffed. "If you haven't asked to court her after this many years, what makes you think you were going to do it today?"

Huffing, William said, "Because I was," he claimed.

"So... go after her," the driver challenged.

"Well, I can't now," William complained. "I've gone and lost my nerve."

Mr. Smithton grimaced. "There's something to be said for already being married," he remarked as he returned his wet hat to his head. "As for you, there's always next year," he added before he led them out the back door and to the stable, all while rain continued to soak the grounds.

CHAPTER 5
TEA TIME PROVES
ENLIGHTENING

eanwhile, in the study

Knowing it would be some time before his daughter would appear for tea, Adam dared a glance at the next sheet in the stack of papers that were now piled on his desk.

A news-sheet from Torquay.

It took him a moment to discover the reason for its inclusion with the other papers, but he finally found an announcement of his grandparents' marriage near the bottom of the page.

The next parchment was the marriage certificate, and below that, he found his father's birth record. He was in the middle of reading the particulars when Connors appeared with a round side table. "Where would you like this, sir?"

Adam surveyed the study and finally pointed to an area in front of the fireplace. "Is there a chair of some sort that will work with it?"

Before Connors could answer, another footman appeared with a small chair. Although it was intended for an adult, it would suit for Penelope's use.

Once the servants were finished, they disappeared and Adam returned his attention to the birth record. So engrossed was he in reading about his father, he missed the arrival of Penelope and didn't even notice that she stood in front of his desk until he reached for the next sheet in the stack.

"Oh!" he said as he quickly came to his feet. "I didn't hear you come in, Poppet."

Penelope performed a perfect curtsy, the hem of her pink gown nearly touching the Axminster carpeting that covered the study floor. "How do, sir?" she said as she extended her hand.

Adam stepped out from the behind the desk and kissed the back of her knuckles several times until she giggled. "You're looking very lovely this afternoon," he said.

"Harris said you wished to see me," she said, her manner not at all expected of an almost-six-year-old. "Is anything wrong?"

Wincing, Adam quickly shook his head. "I

wondered if you might join me for tea is all?" he asked as he waved to the small table. He turned and picked up the tea tray, surprised at how heavy it was. He placed it in the middle of the table, grimacing when it extended beyond the edge of the table top.

"It would be my honor, sir," she happily replied as she once again curtsied and then made her way to the tea set. Appearing both excited and nervous, she kept her attention on him as she climbed onto the chair and then straightened her skirts.

"You can call me 'father'," he replied, pulling his own chair over to sit across from her. "May I pour you a cup?"

"I can do it," she replied, frowning when she noticed he already had his tea.

"I… uh... I thought to invite you when I noticed there were two slices of cake," he stammered. "And an extra cup and saucer."

She nodded her understanding as she stirred milk into her tea and then sat back with the saucer in one hand and the cup of tea in the other. "How are you on this rainy afternoon?" she asked, her ladylike manner quite at odds with her stature.

Adam blinked. "Uh, I'm good. I'm learning some family history, in fact. About your great-grandfather," he said as he indicated the boxes on his desk. "And you? You're looking rather well."

"Thank you, Father. I am, although I was hoping to spend some time out-of-doors today."

"As was I, but I fear we would both drown," he replied. "Would you like a slice of cake?"

"Yes, please."

He set about placing the cake on a small plate and set it aside for her. "I understand you're about to have your own playhouse."

"Indeed," she replied, her missing bottom teeth apparent. "Thanks to Charlotte. She's been such a good friend, Father."

Adam blinked. Had he missed a few of his daughter's birthdays? Her words certainly didn't sound like those of a six-year-old. She seemed taller, too. "May I inquire as to your age?" he asked.

"I am five. Almost six. And although it's probably acceptable for *you* to ask me such a question, I would suggest you not do so with any other woman of your acquaintance." She said the last word in individual syllables, as if she had just learned how to pronounce it.

Adam stared at his daughter. "Understood," he replied. "Where is my daughter, and what have you done with her?"

Penelope's shoulders rose as her head dipped between them. "I've been reading, Father. Learning to read. Mrs. Longburn is such a good teacher. Such a good friend. Thank you for allowing her to see to my education."

Clearing his throat, Adam wondered if he should disabuse his daughter of the idea that he'd had anything to do whatsoever with what Charlotte Longburn was doing on her behalf.

He certainly hadn't had any say in the matter. The woman had simply entered their lives and had been seeing to Penelope's education. Hiring Charlotte Longburn as the girl's governess in an effort to compensate the woman for her time seemed the most logical course of action. Having learned from Harris that a new parson had arrived in Cockington months ago—Adam hadn't attended church since his wife's death—Adam realized Mrs. Longburn's living situation was at risk. He certainly didn't want the widow forced from her home, or worse, forced to marry another parson.

"You're welcome," he replied in response to his daughter's comment.

The sound of Harris' throat clearing had Adam turning to see the butler standing nervously at the door. "Yes?"

"Sir, you have a caller. A Mr. Trayfor."

Adam's eyes widened. "*Michael* Trayfor?" he asked as he stood from his chair. He gave Penelope a quick glance. "Pardon me, Poppet." He turned back to Harris. "I'll need another cup and saucer and more cake," he ordered as he passed the servant and stopped short in the hall upon seeing his caller standing in the vestibule.

"Well, you needn't look as if you've seen a ghost," Michael said as his beefy fists went to his hips.

"Well, that's what it feels like," Adam said as he regarded his friend from his university days. Although it was still pouring rain outside, the man's black attire appeared relatively dry. He hurried up to the taller, larger man and shook his hand. That's when he noticed the man wore a collar rather than a cravat. "What's this?"

"You're looking at Cockington's current parson," Michael replied. "Which you would know if you ever attended a Sunday service," he added on a sigh.

Adam winced as he waved a hand toward the study. "I haven't exactly been very happy with God these past few years," he replied. "And I had no idea you were Longburn's replacement," he added, wondering how he had missed the announcement. He had no doubt been out of town when it happened.

"I was beginning to think I would never get this assignment," Michael said as he glanced around the hall, as if he were attempting to memorize all the details.

Adam shook his head. "I didn't know you wanted it," he said as he led them into his study. "Or I might have been able to pull some strings—"

"It's my fault for not having contacted you back when I decided I wanted to come this far south," Michael said. He paused when he noticed they weren't alone. "Good day, m'lady," he said as he bowed.

Penelope was quick to stand and then held her skirts out to the side as she curtsied. "How do, sir?"

Michael glanced over at Adam, his eyes widening with humor.

"Miss Penelope, may I introduce my good friend Mr. Trayfor? He's our new parson," Adam said, wincing when she grinned. He still wasn't used to seeing her without her bottom teeth.

"It's very good to meet you, sir. Will you join us for tea? I can ring for more cake," Penelope offered.

"I'd like that, actually," Michael replied, moving to the chair next to hers.

Harris appeared with a silver salver loaded with biscuits and cake and another cup and saucer. Penelope's eyes widened at seeing the cake already being delivered when she hadn't yet lifted the bell to ring it. Given the lack of space on the table, the butler saw to transferring the items onto the original tea tray and took his leave. "How do you take your tea, sir?" she asked.

Michael dared another glance in Adam's direction, struggling to hide a grin before he said, "A little milk. Sugar, if you have it."

As Adam joined them, pushing his desk chair so it was across from his caller, Michael watched the young girl prepare his tea. "You look as if you've been hosting tea for some time," he remarked.

"My governess, Mrs. Longburn, taught me."

Michael jerked. "Parson Longburn's widow?" he asked, his gaze turning back to Adam.

Adam placed a slice of cake on a plate and offered it to Michael. "The very same," he said, rolling his eyes. "I didn't realize that by offering her the position and encouraging her to take an apartment here at Wilson Hall also meant that living quarters would become available for *you*," he added. "I suppose you're making arrangements to move into the parsonage now?"

Michael shook his head. "Well, I took a room at the boarding house when I moved to Cockington," he replied, as if he hadn't considered an alternative. "I didn't wish for the widow to have to move on my account."

"The board house is still operating?" Adam asked in surprise. "I thought Mrs. Barrows died."

His brows rising, Michael said, "She did, but her

niece, Barbara, inherited the house. Are you still in the textile business?"

"I am," Adam affirmed. "Which means I've been spending entirely too much time traveling and not enough time here in Cockington." He gave a slight wave in Penelope's direction, as if to indicate she was the reason he was there at all.

"Do you still live in London on occasion?"

Adam shook his head. "Not since..." His gaze once again settled on his daughter.

Michael sobered. "I only recently learned your wife had died. I'm so sorry."

"Six years now," Adam acknowledged.

"But... you've no doubt remarried?" Michael's eyes darted toward Penelope, who seemed to be listening intently to their conversation.

Adam cleared his throat. "No, but it's interesting you should bring up that particular topic. After going through some of my grandfather's papers earlier today, I realize it's time I take another wife. Sire an heir and all," he said with little enthusiasm.

"May I ask as to whom you might be courting?" Penelope asked.

His teacup halfway to his mouth, Adam held it still and stared at his daughter. "Courting?" he repeated.

"Well, don't you have to court a lady before you can

take her to wife?" she asked. She took a sip of tea, her pinky finger appropriately extended.

"Uh, usually," he replied, his hesitance apparent.

"Did you court my mother?"

Before Adam could answer, Michael scoffed. "Your father didn't have to," he offered. "He and your mother were destined to marry one another from the time they met," he claimed. "They were very much in love."

Adam gave a start. "That's true," he acknowledged, quickly setting his saucer on the tray. He feared he might dump the contents on the carpet. "Or, at least, I always knew I was going to marry her," he stammered.

"You did?" Penelope's eyes were round with wonder.

"As Mr. Trayfor said, I loved your mother. Very much. Always did. From the moment I met her," he claimed, clearing his throat when the familiar sensation of sorrow was about to overwhelm him.

About to take a bite of her cake, Penelope paused her fork in midair. "What happened to her?"

Adam grimaced. "She died, Poppet."

Penelope stared at the piece of cake. "So, she didn't just... leave us?"

His brows furrowing, Adam stared at his daughter a moment before he shook his head. "No, dear heart. She didn't have a choice."

Penelope frowned. "Mrs. Longburn says her very best friend left and is never coming back."

Straightening in his chair, Adam wondered at the comment. He gave the parson an apologetic glance and was about to respond when Michael asked, "Who was her very best friend?"

"Her name was Alice," Penelope replied.

"Alice?" Adam repeated, now on the edge of his chair. Had Charlotte had told his daughter about her mother? About them being friends? What else might she had told the tyke?

Penelope nodded, her fork still held in mid-air.

"Alice... as in your mother?" he prompted. He had been married to Alice Winthorpe Wilson for nearly two years when she had given birth to their daughter. She had died the following day.

Nodding again, Penelope finally ate the piece of cake off the end of her fork.

"Is she saying Mrs. Longburn and your late wife knew one another?" Michael asked in a low voice. "In London?"

Adam nodded. "I knew they *knew* one another," he murmured, attempting to hide his alarm. "I suppose I even knew they were… friends," he admitted. His gaze darted to the cartons still on his desk before it settled on the one he had put on the floor. The name 'Alice' was written on the side of it. Although he hadn't yet opened it, he realized he had best do so.

"Did you ever court Mrs. Longburn?" Penelope asked.

Adam blinked. "No, of course not. I barely knew her when I lived in London. Besides, I only ever courted your mother."

Penelope took a sip of tea before her blonde brows wrinkled. "Do all men court their wives before they marry them?"

Relieved the topic was no longer Alice, Adam said, "Your great-grandfather certainly didn't."

Her eyes rounded. "Oh?" she replied. "Then how did he know who to marry?"

Adam allowed a shrug before he reached over and lifted the fair announcement from the pile of papers on his desk. "He held a contest during the local village fair to find his wife," he said as he showed her the flyer and then passed it to Michael.

The parson took the paper from him and read the text, "A rather unusual manner in which to acquire a wife," he commented with a grin.

"It is," Adam agreed. "But expeditious." From the way Penelope's blonde brows furrowed again, he knew he had come up with a word she didn't know. "Effi-cient," he clarified.

"But... did he *love* her?" Penelope asked.

Doing his best to suppress a chuckle, Michael dipped his head and cleared his throat.

Remembering what Connors, the footman, had said and what he had read in that initial stack of papers, Adam nodded. "He did. So much so, he had anything that reminded him of her removed to the attic after she died," he explained. "Which is why all that nice furniture and those boxes were upstairs." *Including the one marked 'Alice'*, but he didn't put voice to the thought.

"In the ballroom, you mean?" Penelope asked.

Adam gave a start. "Well, it might have been at one time." He still wasn't convinced any balls had actually taken place on the fourth floor.

"Oh, but it was," Penelope insisted. "But since Lady Wilson loved to host balls, Lord Wilson made sure no more dancing took place up there after she died," she added.

His eyes darting to the desk, Adam asked, "How is it you know that, Poppet?"

"Mrs. Longburn told me," his daughter said proudly. "She said her husband told her. He knew because he was already alive when it happened," she added, her teacup clutched between her hands.

His eyes rounding, Adam gave his head a shake. "Mayhap when he was a *boy*," he countered, thinking of how many years it had been since his grandparents lived at Wilson Hall.

"A young boy, actually," Penelope agreed. "He used to live in Cockington when he was little, like me. He remembered everything and told Charlotte the stories after they were married. But only during dinner. He didn't talk much to her otherwise."

Michael's look of confusion had Adam rolling his eyes. "Ambrose Longburn was old enough to be his wife's... grandfather, I think," he explained.

"Ah," Michael replied. "This somewhat explains why he wanted the position here in Cockington. A return to the home of his youth," he murmured. "Tell me, were Mrs. Longburn and your Alice about the same age?"

"Indeed," Adam acknowledged before he pointed to the flyer that Michael still held. "Don't you think holding a contest is a rather... *scandalous* way in which to acquire a wife?"

Michael shook his head. "As you said, it was... efficient."

"Efficient," Penelope repeated, struggling to say the word given her lack of bottom teeth. "Is that what you're going to do to find your next wife, Father? Hold a contest? I would really like a mother."

Chiming in with his own opinion, Michael said,

"You are in need of an heir, and you're not going to sire one unless you take a wife."

Adam's mouth dropped open. "You're suggesting I hold a contest at the village fair to find a *wife*?"

Penelope's face brightened. "Why, Father. What an excellent idea."

Finally allowing the chuckle he'd been holding in, Michael said, "I'll be sure to let the villagers know you thought of it," he said with a grin. He indicated the flyer he still held. "However, might I suggest you allow widows to apply? You would miss out on some rather excellent options should you exclude them," he added.

"Widows?" Adam repeated.

"In fact, I believe you should allow any woman who is not currently married to enter the contest," Michael added, as if he were daring his friend to move ahead with the idea.

Adam had to suppress the urge to throttle the parson. He felt as if he was being set up. "All right," he hedged. He turned his attention on his daughter. "You do realize you could end up with a complete stranger for a mother?" he warned. From the look of alarm that appeared on Penelope's face, Adam grimaced. "What is it?"

"I am quite sure I have met every woman in the village, Father," she replied.

The parson chuckled. "I rather doubt there will be as many for you to consider as your grandfather had to choose from," he remarked. "Unless you advertise it more widely. Mayhap include Torquay and Livermead when you put out your flyers," he teased as he held up the faded sheet.

"True," Adam acknowledged, ignoring the parson's jibe. If the advertisement didn't reach Torquay, there would be only two unmarried women and one widow eligible to apply. If the news of the contest reached Torquay and beyond, there might be dozens of young women to consider. "Should I put an age limit on it?" he asked, intending the parson to answer.

But Penelope's brows wrinkled. "No. Any and all young ladies should be allowed to enter," she stated. "They just have to be able to have children."

This time, Adam couldn't help but chuckle at her pronouncement. Then he quickly sobered. "What if I don't *like* any of them?" he asked, a look of doubt crossing his face.

Giving him a quelling glance, Penelope angled her head to one side and said, "There will be at least *one* we both like, Father."

Michael held a hand in front of his mouth to hide his grin. "From the mouths of babes," he whispered.

Wishing he had spiked his tea from the bottle of

brandy behind his desk, Adam finished off his cup of tea and regarded his daughter with a quirked brow. "All right, Poppet. A contest at the annual village fair it shall be," he said, resisting the urge to grimace.

"I'm going to tell Mrs. Longburn right now," Penelope said as she stood. Caught off-guard, Adam and Michael struggled to gain their own feet. Although Penelope tried to curtsy, Adam slipped his hands beneath her arms and lifted her into the air. She squealed in delight as he settled her on his hip and kissed the side of her head.

"How is it you've grown so tall?" he asked with a sigh.

"I eat everything on my plate," she replied, her fists wrapping around his neck as her head ended up on his shoulder.

Adam dared a glance down at the tea tray, finding that she had, indeed, eaten her entire slice of cake. "Tell me, Poppet, what were you doing when Harris told you to come down for tea?"

Penelope gave his question some thought before she said, "Helping Mrs. Longburn."

He frowned. "Doing what?"

"Setting up my new playroom."

"Ah, of course," he replied. "Well, I suppose you'd

best join her. Do come down for dinner with me later, won't you?"

Penelope nodded. "May I bring Mrs. Longburn?"

Adam was about to reply in the negative, but noticed his daughter's look of concern. "Why do want her at dinner?"

"I don't like eating alone."

He gave a start. "Well, you won't be eating alone if you're eating with me," he replied.

She screwed up her face in a grimace. "But if I'm eating with you, *she* will be eating alone. I don't want her to have to eat alone."

Touched by his daughter's concern for another, he said, "Well, then we'll ask her to join us."

Although the very last guest he wanted at dinner was a managing female, he decided he could make it through a meal in Mrs. Longburn's company. He could spend part of the meal imagining what she might look like with her hair down, or how she might appear in the early morning hours after a night of spirited lovemaking, or how she might sound in the throes of ecstasy. It took only seconds for him to realize he had best stop thinking of the governess or his arousal would become apparent.

"Thank you, Father," she replied, giving him a kiss

on his cheek. She turned her attention to the parson. "It's very good to meet you, sir."

"You as well, Miss Penelope," Michael replied, suppressing his smirk.

"Off you go," Adam said as he lowered Penelope until her feet touched the floor. He watched as she hurried out of his office and then heard her greet Harris before she made her way up the stairs.

Returning to his guest, Adam gave him a quelling glance when he saw the man's look of amusement. "Just you wait until you have a daughter," he warned.

Chuckling, the parson placed a hand over his chest. "You're very good with her," he said. "Most aristocrats meet their daughters when they're born and then not again until they're having their come-out," he added as he watched Adam stand on the study's threshold. The baronet's attention was still on his retreating daughter as she climbed the stairs.

"Well, I'm not an aristocrat. Not really," Adam replied as he returned to his seat and took up his plate of cake.

Michael angled his head to one side. "I can't help but think you're not happy with having Mrs. Longburn in your household. Why is that?"

Adam gave a start before he shook his head. "It's nothing, really. We met a long time ago, in London, and

I'm not sure if I said something, or if she did, but we never seemed to get on after that. So imagine my shock when I learned that she and her father had shown up here in Cockington with Longburn in tow."

"Imagine mine when I learned Longburn got the position I was in line for," Michael countered with an arched brow.

Adam remembered what the parson had said out in the vestibule. "So you wanted the position here back then?" Adam asked in surprise. "That was... what, four years ago?"

"I did," Michael replied with a nod. "Patience is a virtue it seems. I was about to lose it, though, when Longburn died and they still didn't let me have it right away. Had to wait until my replacement was lined up in Cornwall."

Adam nodded his understanding. "So... you find Cockington agreeable?"

Michael grinned. "I do, actually," he replied. He pulled a chronometer from waistcoat pocket and glanced at it. "And I best get back to my room at the boarding house. I have a sermon to write for Sunday's service and Easter after that," he claimed.

"Well, I appreciate your call," Adam said as he stood. "And your patience with my daughter. I probably should have had her nursemaid come collect her—"

"No," Michael interrupted as he held up a staying hand. "She's a beautiful girl," he remarked as they made their way to the vestibule. "And I sometimes think children teach us some very valuable lessons we might have at one time known but have long since forgotten."

Adam furrowed his brows as he considered the parson's words. "You sounded very wise just then," he commented.

"I should. I'm man of the cloth," Michael replied with a grin.

They said their farewells, and Adam watched as Michael step into a covered curricle pulled by a familiar looking Friesian. Even if he hadn't moved into the parsonage, it seemed the parson had at least made off with the equipage and horse that belonged to it.

When Adam made his way back to his study, his gaze fell on his grandfather's advertisement. He mentally calculated the time until the village fair was due to take place.

If the usual organizers, Mrs. Baker and Mrs. Stafford, were involved, they would schedule it for the first regular market day following Easter, which meant it would be held in only ten days.

Lifting the advertisement from the tray, he reread the words in an effort to decide how best to update it for the upcoming contest. It seemed a flyer would be required.

He would see to it after he helped himself to a brandy.

CHAPTER 6
A DINNER LEADS TO
ASSUMPTIONS

*L*ater that evening

Informed by her charge that she was expected to join Sir Adam and his daughter for dinner that night, Charlotte dropped the book she'd been reading aloud into her lap and stared at the girl. "Are you quite sure?"

Penelope nodded. "I had tea with Father and his friend Mr. Trayfor this morning," she replied. "I should have told you earlier, but I forgot."

Charlotte gave a start at hearing the parson had paid a call. "Mr. Trayfor is a friend of your father's?" she asked.

"From uversity," the young girl acknowledged, although she seemed to realize she had said the word incorrectly. "What's uversity?"

"University," Charlotte said. "School for older students."

"Will I go to university?"

Angling her head to one side, Charlotte sighed. "They don't accept girls at university," she replied. "However, you'll probably go to finishing school when I've done as much as I can," she added, wondering if she would last in her position long enough to see that happen.

The rest of what Penelope had said about dinner had her glancing at her chronometer. She winced when she noted the time. Changing her gown for something more appropriate to wear to dinner wouldn't take long, but she hadn't exactly done up her hair into more than a simple messy bun atop her head that morning. "Do you know what time dinner is to be served?"

Furrowing her brows, Penelope said, "When the little hand is on the number seven." She was about to point to Charlotte's chronometer with a pudgy finger, but stopped and pulled it back. "Where are the numbers?" she asked in dismay.

Given the pocket watch's numbers were Roman numerals, Charlotte immediately understood Penelope's query. "Someday I'll teach you how to read these sorts of numbers," she promised. "But if dinner is at seven…" She pointed to the VII. "Then we really must see to changing our clothes." She lifted the girl from her lap and stood. "I'll see you to the nursery."

The nursemaid appeared to take Penelope in hand while Charlotte hurried to her apartment. Given it was on the same floor as the nursery, she didn't have to go far.

She did have to dig through a trunk for an appropriate gown, however. Although she had brought the trunks to the house the day before, she hadn't yet taken the time to unpack more than her day gowns.

Donning the least wrinkled of her dinner gowns, Charlotte spent a moment regarding her reflection in the dressing table mirror. She leaned in closer, grimacing when she noticed a few sunspots on her nose. With all the rain that had fallen the past few days, she hadn't been out of doors for more than the time she had driven to and from the parsonage. What had caused freckles to suddenly appear?

Once she had her hair redone in a simple but elegant chignon, she located her pots of cosmetics in her valise and saw to covering the spots on her nose and at the top of her cheeks. When the clock on the mantel chimed seven times, she made her way to the nursery to collect Penelope.

Sir Adam was already there, though, bent down to

greet his daughter with his usual teasing kisses on the back on her proffered hand.

"Father," she giggled in delight. She caught sight of Charlotte and curtsied. "You look pretty," she said as she escaped her father's hold to join her governess at the door.

"Why, thank you. As do you," Charlotte said as she deliberately avoided the baronet's stare. It was obvious he hadn't changed clothes for dinner, and now she felt terribly overdressed. At least Penelope's nursemaid had seen to dressing her in what appeared to be her Sunday best.

"We should go down now," Adam said as he captured his daughter's hand in his. He turned his attention back to Charlotte. "You really didn't have to change clothes," he murmured. "We're not in London any longer."

Inhaling softly, Charlotte realized then that he had remembered meeting her in the capital. "I wasn't aware of the protocols for dinner here at Wilson Hall," she replied.

"We're practically in the country here," he said. "I trust your day has gone as expected?" he asked as they made their way down to the dining room, each of them gripping one of Penelope's hands so she was between them.

Charlotte nodded. "Indeed. I believe we'll begin using the new classroom upstairs in a couple of days."

"That soon?" He frowned, apparently not expecting it would be ready.

"Your servants seem as anxious to see to its completion as Miss Penelope is," Charlotte remarked as Connors held a chair for her at the table. She took the seat and watched as Adam helped Penelope into another. Once he took his place at the carver, Mrs. McNulty appeared with a soup tureen and served while the footman saw to pouring wine.

"We haven't had anything change here at Wilson Hall in a long time," he replied. Although the words seemed pleasant enough, he appeared troubled.

The dinner continued and seemed pleasant enough, although their topics of conversation were meant to include Penelope and so they didn't touch on anything of a personal nature.

"I do hope you're not terribly upset about the ballroom," Charlotte hedged. "I didn't intend for it to cause this much disruption in the household."

"Not at all," he replied between bites of his roast beef, his words sounding sincere. "I'm rather glad you thought of it." After a pause, he glanced over at his daughter. "I suppose it's merely the start for far more changes," he stated, before returning his attention to his meal.

Charlotte had no idea what he meant by the rest of his comment and had to resist the urge to ask, "What changes?"

Adam once again regarded his daughter, this time with a thoughtful gaze. "I would do anything for Miss Penelope, now that you have made her the lady of the house."

Penelope's eyes widened in surprise. "The lady of the house?" she repeated with a huge grin. "Me?"

"Yes, you," he replied. "Now that you know how to host a small dinner party and serve tea, I shall expect you to be my hostess when I host callers or invite colleagues for dinner," he said.

From the dour manner in which he made the comment, Charlotte was quite sure he was serious. Then she caught his quick glance and wink in her direction, and she relaxed.

Penelope, on the other hand, beamed in delight and asked Charlotte if she could assist her in coming up with suitable menus for business dinners.

Both Adam and Charlotte had blinked before Charlotte assured the girl she would indeed help with such an endeavor.

"They grow up so fast," Adam murmured then, his

gaze resting on Charlotte a few seconds too long before he returned his attention to his meal.

It was at that moment when a frisson passed through Charlotte, one that nearly had her gasping in surprise.

How could the baronet's simple comment incite such a response? Have her feeling tingly all over and suddenly uncomfortable in his presence?

When he took his port at the table instead of retiring to his study, Charlotte noticed Penelope about to fall asleep in what was left of her dessert course. "I'll take her up to the nursery," Charlotte murmured before she dipped a curtsy and escorted the youngster to the door.

Rising to his feet, Adam said, "I'll be up in a moment to tuck you in."

Although she knew his words were meant for his daughter, Charlotte was well aware of him watching her as she led Penelope out of the room. The thought of having him tuck her in for the night left her near breathless as she climbed the stairs.

CHAPTER 7
A CONTEST IS DISCUSSED

*T*wo *days later, the Cockington village square*

"If I wasn't already married, I would enter," Mrs. Stafford said as she read the notice that was posted in the window of the village's only mercantile.

"You wouldn't be eligible," Mrs. Baker accused as she pointed to the clause at the end of the announcement.

Only unmarried women of childbearing age are eligible.

The mother of two unmarried tenant farmers, the stout woman gave her friend an assessing glance. "It says you have to be able to have children."

Mrs. Stafford, a bit taller than her friend and far more buxom, frowned and then sniffed. "How would the baronet know?" she asked before she finally grinned to show she wasn't serious. "One thing is for certain. This along with the lamb competition will help attract more people to the village fair this year."

As one of the organizers of the annual market day fair, she had already begun her part in soliciting the usual vendors while Mrs. Baker, her co-organizer, was lining up participants for the baked goods and early vegetables competitions.

Mrs. Stafford greeted one of the store clerks as they entered the shop. "What do you know of this?" she asked of Theodore Coulsden.

The older brother of the Wilson Hall groom, William, Theodore seemed surprised at being asked his opinion. He gave a shrug. "Don't know that I do. Mrs. McNulty asked that I post it when she was in earlier today. Just finally had a chance to actually read it a few minutes ago."

Mrs. Baker sniffed as she exchanged glances with Mrs. Stafford. "Seems a rather scandalous way in which to acquire a wife," she remarked.

The clerk, whose pate was nearly bald, had cheeks that sagged as if they no longer had any bones from which to hang, angled his head to one side. "Worked for Sir Adam's grandfather," he countered.

"His grandfather?" Mrs. Baker repeated in surprise. She moved closer to the counter, as did Mrs. Stafford.

"Aye. A bit before your time, but that's how the third baronet found his wife," Theodore claimed. "Women came from all over Devonshire to enter, including one Miss Gertrude Amherst. Right proper girl she was. Sang like a dove, too," he claimed. "She made for a very fine Lady Wilson." When he noted how the two matrons before him didn't seem convinced, the lanky man added, "The current baronet is a busy man. Prob'ly doesn't have time to court a lady."

Both of the women inhaled softly. "I cannot imagine," Mrs. Baker said in a quiet voice. "That particular Lady Wilson was always so... so proper. A real lady she was."

"As was the current baronet's mother," Mrs. Stafford argued. "Such a tragedy, the way she and the fourth baronet died of cholera, and all because she insisted they go to London for the Season. Didn't even get to see their son marry Alice Winthorpe, God rest her soul."

"Oh, but they knew he would wed her eventually," Mrs. Baker countered. "That's one marriage that was foretold from the time those two lovebirds met as children." Her gloved hands clasped together as she sighed.

Although Mrs. Baker hadn't actually met the baronet's late wife, she had been privy to gossip about the couple on her only two visits to the capital.

"Well, the third Lady Wilson was always good to me father," Theodore said as he pointed to the flyer. "Saw to it he had a position as a secretary. My brother was hired as a stable boy," he added before his brows furrowed. "Which has me wondering if the winner of this contest will be anything like her. Don't want no snooty miss from London winnin', if you catch my meaning."

Mrs. Stafford sniffed. "If that happens, Sir Adam won't be staying here in Cockington," she claimed. "Mark my words. Any wife from the city will have him living in London year 'round."

"If that happens, who will see to posting the reward for the best lamb in the annual competition?" Mrs. Baker asked with worry.

"Who will be living in London year 'round?"

The two older women turned in unison to see Charlotte Longburn stepping into the mercantile.

"Sir Adam," Mrs. Baker replied before she exchanged quick glances with her friend. "You did see the advertisement in the window?" she half-asked.

Charlotte shook her head before she followed their gazes to the flyer. She plucked it from its perch in the window and read it, her brows rising in shock. "Oh, dear," she whispered. "He must have found his grandfather's papers," Charlotte murmured. She rolled her eyes, remembering the cartons that had been up in the old ballroom. The ones marked as belonging to the third baronet Wilson.

From what her late husband had told her about that particular baronet, Charlotte had thought the third baronet of Cockington mad. That he had managed to secure a suitable wife from holding a contest at the village fair seemed an unlikely prospect, but stories of Lady Gertrude Wilson had the woman pegged as the perfect wife and lady. "This is all my fault," Charlotte murmured on a sigh.

A collective gasp answered her comment. "What are you talking about?" Mrs. Baker asked.

Charlotte rolled her eyes. "I'm quite sure Sir Adam wouldn't have learned about his grandfather's contest except that I asked that the old ballroom in Wilson Hall be cleaned out to make a playroom for his daughter. He must have found a contest flyer in one of the boxes they took down to his study."

Once the two footmen had cleared out the fourth floor of Wilson Hall, Mrs. McNulty had the upstairs maids clean the ballroom. Earlier that morning, footmen moved in some reupholstered furniture, and the Wilson Hall laundress was washing the curtain panels. Charlotte expected she and Penelope would be using it as a classroom and a playroom within a day or two.

"So, it's true," Mrs. Stafford said, exchanging glances with Mrs. Baker again. "You've taken a position at Wilson Hall?"

Charlotte nodded, curious as to how the villagers had already learned of it. She had only told the servants at the parsonage, but she supposed Kate and Eloise would have been quick to spread the news. "I have. As Miss Penelope's governess," she admitted. "I've already begun my duties, of course, but I have errands that must be done whilst the girl is napping."

The two matrons exchanged quick glances before Mrs. Baker remarked, "Well, it's about time you be paid for what you have already been doing for that poor girl."

Relieved the older woman didn't find fault with the new arrangement, Charlotte winced when Mrs. Stafford took the opposite stance.

"Governess? Why, is that even allowed? A *paid* position? You're the widow of a parson," the older matron stated.

"I am, yes," Charlotte admitted, realizing she would forever be known as a parson's widow. "But I'm not dead yet," she added, catching the sympathetic eye of Mr. Coulsden. "I am in need of some ribbon. Three yards should do it," she said.

"A new gown?" Mrs. Baker asked, a brow arched suggestively.

"One to wear for the contest?" Mrs. Stafford queried, her teasing tone suggesting she had completely forgotten her stance on Charlotte becoming a governess.

"The contest?" Charlotte repeated. She still held the flyer in her gloved hand.

"You *are* going to enter?" Theodore Coulsden queried. "All women of marriageable age are eligible," he added. "Even widows."

Charlotte was about to reply in the negative, but she glanced at the flyer once more. She was certainly of an appropriate age. Her mourning period was over. And she did rather like the thought of Miss Penelope as a stepdaughter as opposed to simply her charge.

As for becoming the wife of Sir Adam Wilson, well, she was fairly sure she could abide the handsome man's company. He was polite and smelled good and always dressed in the very best superfine woolens. There were other considerations as well, such as his dark blue eyes.

At times, they seemed filled with mirth while at others, they appeared almost haunted. Her fingers itched to comb through his dark brown hair. She was sure it was as silky as it appeared under candle light.

At one point in her past, she had imagined him courting her instead of Alice. It hadn't seemed so unlikely back in London, even though Alice and Adam had been childhood sweethearts.

But could Adam abide her? For the short amount of time they had known one another in London—how could she not have been at least an acquaintance of Alice Winthrop's betrothed?—Charlotte had never had the impression Adam did more than tolerate her very existence. As if her status as Alice's best friend was a threat to their inevitable marriage. But why should her friendship with Alice have to end simply because she was marrying Sir Adam Wilson?

Even now, Charlotte wasn't sure the baronet even liked her. From the moment they had first met in London, she had the impression the man despised her. Perhaps she had merely imagined the cut indirect, but then, she hadn't been happy to learn her best friend would be marrying the man Alice had always said she would marry.

Marry and have a child who would result in her death.

. . .

Charlotte turned her attention back to the flyer. "Tell me, Mrs. Stafford. Aren't you in charge of the village fair?"

"I am," the older woman acknowledged proudly, her bosom rising a few inches as she straightened. "With Mildred, of course," she added, referring to Mrs. Baker. "Been doing it for... oh, twenty years or so. This year's fair is only eight days away."

Charlotte regarded the two matrons with a furrowed brow. "Will you be taking charge of this particular contest?"

The older women both glanced at one another a moment before they shook their heads. "Don't see how I'll have the time given my attentions must be on lining up the market vendors," Mrs. Stafford remarked.

"And I'll be in charge of the contests for the baked goods and early vegetables," Mrs. Baker chimed in.

"We've added a contest for the best lambs seeing as how Sir Adam will be donating the prize money for the winner," Mrs. Stafford added. "Never done that before."

Charlotte nodded her understanding. "The advertisement doesn't say where or how to apply," she commented.

The matrons both shrugged.

"I suppose the baronet just expects the contestants to show up at the fair," the clerk said. "Much as they did the last time. There was a table where they listed their age and qualifications," he explained. "But from the way this flyer is worded, I think the eligible ladies just have to report to the stage at noon at the fair."

"The stage?" Mrs. Baker repeated, her eyes widening in alarm. "That assumes there will *be* a stage."

"Or a place for the contestants to gather," Charlotte suggested.

"Oh, a stage isn't a problem," Mrs. Baker remarked with a wave of a gloved hand. "I can have my boys build it," she offered.

"Rebuild, you mean," Mrs. Stafford said. "Remember, we had them build one last year when we had that pie eating contest. A mess, that was," she added, shuddering. "Berries everywhere. I think the boards are still stained from it, but the stage can easily be reconstructed."

"She's right," Mrs. Baker said. "Both my boys entered that contest. Took a fortnight for my laundress to get the stains out of their shirts."

"My son ate all of Miss Sherman's lemon pies, so it wasn't so bad," Mrs. Stafford added. "Although Elijah looked as if he'd swallowed a particularly sour lemon for three weeks afterwords."

Having been present for the last pie eating contest, Charlotte remembered how puckered Elijah's cheeks had looked as he managed to consume four entire lemon pies. He had only lost the contest because Bobby Baker had eaten five berry pies in the same amount of time. Although she was sure Elijah didn't particularly enjoy the lemon pies, he had married Miss Sherman the following month.

"So, the stage could be rebuilt for the Lady Wilson contest?" Charlotte asked, hoping to get the women back on topic.

"Oh, yes," Mrs. Stafford assured her. "Elijah can do it with the Baker boys." Her eyes widened. "Besides, we'll need it for the jugglers and sword swallowers."

Charlotte blinked. "Sword swallowers?" she repeated, resisting the urge to gulp and swallow. She didn't remember seeing them at the fair the year before.

"They are a part of a traveling troupe who entertains at the county fairs," Mrs. Baker explained. "We sent out an invitation and have learned they will just show up and entertain whoever watches them."

Realizing the stage would be indeed be built for the contest, Charlotte considered the other particulars.

"There will need to be a sign of some sort," she mused. "A shingle above the stage."

"My Robert can see to that," Mrs. Baker offered. "He can just paint over the old one he did for the pie eating contest."

"Do you suppose we'll need a curtain? For the women to stand behind until they're ready to be presented?" Mrs. Stafford asked.

Although she hadn't thought of it, Charlotte realized it would be a good idea. She could just imagine a bevy of young women walking about the village fair in search of the contest.

Or Sir Adam.

The three women exchanged quick glances before turning to Theodore Coulsden. His eyes widened before he understood their meaning. "I have a curtain around here somewhere," he acknowledged. "The one that Madame de la Quois stitched together for the play they put on last year in the church," he added.

"You are going to enter?" Mrs. Stafford asked as she turned to regard Charlotte with an arched brow.

"What?" Charlotte's eyes widened in alarm.

"You are eligible, young lady," Mrs. Baker put in. "The flyer doesn't say anything about widows not being allowed."

Charlotte shook her head. "Oh, I rather doubt it would be seemly for me to—"

"Nonsense. You really must. In fact, I think we'll just put *you* in charge of the contest," Mrs. Stafford said with a nod.

Charlotte stared at the matron. Entering a contest to have a chance at becoming Adam Wilson's wife seemed so wrong, but she couldn't help the pleasurable sensation of excitement that skittered down her spine.

The chance to be Lady Wilson. To be Penelope's stepmother.

The thought of sharing Sir Adam's bed had her nipples hardening into tight buds, the space at the top of her thighs tingling with anticipation. Even if Sir Adam was only in Cockington a fortnight every month, they would surely take breakfasts and dinners together when he was home. Share time together with Penelope. Perhaps she and his daughter could even join him on his travels.

"How many women do you suppose will enter this contest?" Charlotte asked, not about to commit to the folly just yet.

Mrs. Baker and Mrs. Stafford both shrugged. Theodore Coulsden grinned, though. "Pro'bly about ten or so, once word gets out to the neighboring towns," he said. "Unless..." He allowed the comment to trail off before he gave a shrug.

"Unless?" Charlotte prompted.

The clerk gave his head a quick shake. "Now what color ribbon were you needin', Mrs. Longburn?"

Charlotte furrowed her brows, realizing Mr. Coulsden wasn't willing to share his thoughts in front of the two busybodies. "Blue, I should think," she replied.

"Good choice. I'll have it ready for you in just a moment."

Charlotte inhaled softly. "Oh, do wait on them first. They were here before me," she said, deciding she wanted to discover what the clerk had been unwilling to say in front of the matrons.

While Mr. Coulsden filled the other women's orders, Charlotte strolled through the mercantile, filling her basket with embroidery thread and yarn, a small pair of scissors, a wooden hoop, and a square of linen. Given the amount of light in the old ballroom, she knew it would be the perfect place to teach Penelope how to embroider.

When the door shut behind Mrs. Stafford and Mrs. Baker, Charlotte took the basket to the counter. Mr. Coulsden stepped up with a roll of blue ribbon and added it to her other items.

"Unless?" Charlotte prompted again.

The clerk grinned, which had his sagging cheeks lifting in a manner that youthened him by more than a decade. "Unless you can see to it you're the only one who enters the contest."

Charlotte blinked. "Me?" she asked in disbelief. "What makes you think I wish to become Lady Wilson?" she asked, well aware her face was bright pink.

Mr. Coulsden's grin widened. "Why, that blush says it all, Mrs. Longburn," he replied with a chuckle.

Embarrassed, Charlotte had a thought to take her leave of the shop—leave her entire purchase on the counter without arranging payment—but she realized the man only wished to help. She pressed her lips together and swallowed. "I suppose you have a suggestion as to how that might be arranged?"

He angled his head from side to side before he leaned over the counter. "Well, someone needs to run the contest. Take the names of all the entrants," he replied. "Find someone to act as the hostess, if you will. Make sure only the obvious winner is entered along with a few who have no chance due to their advanced age or extreme youth."

Charlotte stared at the clerk a moment before her

eyes suddenly widened. "And you're saying that person should be me?" she asked.

"May as well be. Mrs. McNulty brought that flyer in this morning," he replied, pointing to the one Charlotte still held. "She would pro'bly tell you where else they've been distributed."

Charlotte furrowed her brows. "Why would I wish to know that?" she asked, suspicious.

"It helps if the flyers mysteriously disappear," he said in response, a gray bushy eyebrow arching mischievously. "Less chance of anyone else learnin' of the contest."

Charlotte gasped. "Mr. Coulsden," she scolded. "How is it you even know of such things?"

The clerk leaned toward her and said, "Sir Adam's grandmother was my great aunt," he said, his eyes twinkling with mischief.

Charlotte's eyes rounded in understanding. "And who hosted the contest back then?"

He chuckled. "My mum, of course. Got her sister married to the baronet. Then my father became the baronet's secretary, and my brother was hired as a groom over at the Wilson Hall stables. We're all family through that marriage."

"You're a cousin to Sir Adam?"

"I am. Second cousin, I suppose."

"Does Miss Penelope know she's related to you?" Charlotte asked, curious as to if Sir Adam had introduced her to his relatives.

Scratched his bushy brow with a gnarled finger, Mr. Coulsden frowned. "Don't know that she does," he replied.

Staring at the clerk in disbelief, Charlotte knew in an instant who should play hostess for the contest.

Now she just had to convince Sir Adam that Miss Penelope could handle the job.

CHAPTER 8
CONTRACTS AND CONTESTS

eanwhile, in the study at Wilson Hall Adam read the contract before him and winced. He was sure there was something he was missing. Some detail or clause that would result in financial ruin. Some stipulation that would be impossible to meet.

Dealing with textile manufacturers was usually fraught with unforeseen problems—production delays, Luddites sabotaging equipment, nubbly silk, substandard wool—but this particular contract seemed to account for any and all circumstances that might arise.

He had never done business with Banks Textiles in the past, but he was determined to include their Merino wool in the next offerings at Wilson Drapers in London. Banks Textiles had been successfully producing fabrics from the wool of the Portuguese-based sheep for decades, turning out a deep red wool that had become their trademark product.

For a moment, he imagined Mrs. Longburn wearing a redingote made from the wool. She looked stunning in his mind's eye, her flame-colored hair a perfect compliment to the red outer garment. Decorated with black frog closures down the front and black epaulets at the shoulders, the coat could be worn to the theatre or to a ball, for a walk in Hyde Park or a stroll on The Strand.

Then he imagined Penelope wearing the same style of coat, walking hand-in-hand with her new governess, and he straightened at his desk. He signed both copies of the contract, sighing with relief when the ink was dry enough for him to roll up the documents and slide them into a carrier.

Wilson Drapers would be offering Merino wool before the end of the Season.

A knock at his study door had him glancing up to discover the housekeeper peeking around the opening.

"Yes?"

Mrs. McNulty curtsied. "So sorry to interrupt, sir, but I wanted to let you know that those flyers you asked me to put up about the village have been posted. Over in Livermead, too, sir."

Adam almost asked what flyers she was referring to

when he grimaced. "Oh. Thank you," he replied, now wishing he had never given into the ridiculous idea of finding his next wife by way of a bride contest. "I appreciate you taking the time to do that. Do you suppose any should be hung up over in Torquay?"

The housekeeper stared at him a moment before she leaned into the study and said, "I really don't think you'd want any of the young misses from over there, Sir Adam."

Adam was about to ask why, but decided it best he take up the matter with someone else. He hadn't heard anything untoward about young ladies from Torquay, but then he hadn't been home much in the past year or two. His trips to London and Yorkshire had kept him away from Cockington more than half that time.

Mrs. McNulty stepped into the study and placed a few flyers on the edge of the desk. "Mr. Baker said he printed some extras for you, in the event any get... lost or... or stolen."

Adam leaned back in his chair. "Stolen?" he repeated and then scoffed. "Why ever would anyone steal a flyer?"

The housekeeper shrugged. "The flyers advertising positions get taken all the time, sir, so as others won't know there's a job to apply for," she explained. "Less competition."

Furrowing a brow, Adam tried to imagine a young woman removing the flyers from shop windows lest others learn of the contest to find the next Lady Wilson.

Surely a proper young woman wouldn't stoop to such measures.

Would she?

He had to suppress a chuckle that there might be some sort of jealousy amongst those that planned to enter the competition. He had never considered he might be a catch. Although he could offer a decent home by way of Wilson Hall, and his wife would be styled a lady, he wasn't a member of the aristocracy. He was rarely in London for the Season, so his wife wouldn't be there to attend every ball, soirée, and garden party, even if the hostesses knew enough to invite her.

He was almost afraid to ask his next question. "Where did you end up posting them? Just so I know from where I can expect responses."

Mrs. McNulty pulled a paper from her pocket. "Three here in Cockington. At the mercantile, the butcher's, and at the baker's. One over in Livermead. There's only the mercantile with a window in that village. There is also just the one in Torquay, at the shop where they was printed by Mr. Baker," she recited.

"But..." She paused, her face taking on a look of uncertainty.

"What is it?"

"The flyer doesn't say anything about sending a response, sir."

Adam winced and pulled one of the flyers from the edge of his desk to review it.

Announcing the Lady Wilson Contest

Adam Wilson, 5th Baronet of Cockington, will choose his next wife from those eligible young ladies entered into a contest to become Lady Wilson. Young women must be of marriageable age and free of scandal. Come to the stage at the Cockington village fair at noon!

He grimaced, realizing he really should have had applications sent to Wilson Hall in advance. "Oh, I see what you mean," he murmured, frowning at his blunder. "Well, I suppose we'll just be surprised," he said on a sigh, hoping he didn't sound as frustrated as he felt.

"Very good, sir. Oh, and Mr. Smithton asked if he should put away the coach-and-four, or if you'll be wanting a ride anywhere later today?"

Tempted to deliver the contracts he had just signed

in person, Adam realized it was far too late in the day to start the trip to Darlington, and Darlington was too far away—he'd be gone for almost a fortnight, even if he took the train for part of the journey. Besides, he could send the contracts with a courier or by mail coach. There was no need for him to leave his daughter again so soon.

"I won't be needing the coach," Adam finally replied. "But do send Harris in, won't you? I have papers that need to be sent by the mail coach."

"Yes, sir," the housekeeper said as she dipped a curtsy. She took her leave of the study and set off to find the butler.

As quiet as she could, Charlotte emerged from the ground floor parlor and ducked into the vestibule. Still wearing her redingote and hat from when she had followed Mrs. McNulty into the house, she opened and closed the front door and then slipped out of the coat, pretending as if she had just returned to Wilson Hall.

Overhearing Mrs. McNulty's comment as to where she had posted the flyers for the contest, Charlotte now knew which businesses she would need to visit the following day in order to remove the flyers. Despite the baronet's question about why anyone would do such a thing—she knew exactly why—she was determined to follow through with her plan.

She could only hope they hadn't already been noticed by any desperate widow or unmarried woman.

CHAPTER 9
THE SERVANTS PLOT A PLAN

A few minutes later

As William Coulsden led the coach horses to the large door at one end of the stable, the traveling coach lumbering behind under an incessant drizzle, he was surprised to see Mrs. McNulty emerge from the kitchen and head his way. The manner in which she clutched her skirts in one hand had him gulping. Despite her knit stockings, he could clearly make out her shapely ankles with her every step.

Something else of a different shape was reacting as well, but given he wore his cape coat, he wasn't concerned that it was about to make itself evident.

From her hurried manner, he knew something had happened.

"Why, what is it, Mrs. McNulty?" he asked as he

halted the horses, tipped his hat, and gave a slight bow. At the bottom of the bow, he had to suppress a sigh of disappointment at noticing the housekeeper had let go of her skirts. Her ankles, a source of late night dreams for the groom, were no longer on display.

"I need a word, Mr. Coulsden," she replied as she waved him into the stable and disappeared through the door.

Curious, William urged the horses to resume their trip into the stable. Excitement gripped him at the thought the housekeeper might be there to seek a liaison with him. Since she had spoken with him only moments ago regarding the baronet's orders about the coach and hadn't said anything else, what could she be there to say if not something private? Something only the two of them could share?

Mayhap a kiss in the newest horse stall? Even if it didn't yet have its door installed?

After all these years, perhaps she was the one who would suggest they begin courting.

Once the coach had cleared the large wooden doors, he rushed to shut them and then joined the housekeeper where she was waiting next to one of the stalls.

"Why, Mrs. McNulty..." He paused when he realized Mr. Smithton was standing with the housekeeper. "Mr. Smithton," he acknowledged, unable to hide the disappointment he felt at realizing he wouldn't be alone with Mrs. McNulty.

"Coulsden," Mr. Smithton acknowledged. "What's this about?" he asked, turning his attention back to housekeeper.

Mrs. McNulty leaned in, keeping her voice low. "Those flyers I put up?" she began. "They have to come down."

"What?" William asked in confusion. "But... but you just finished puttin' 'em up." His eyes suddenly rounded. "Did the baronet change his mind about the contest?"

She rolled her eyes. "Unfortunately, no," she replied. "We all know there can be only one woman in that contest to become the baronet's wife," she stated. Her gaze darted between the two of them, as if she was sure they would both know who she was talking about.

Mr. Smithton furrowed his brows. "Are you referring to Mrs. Longburn?"

Giving him a quelling glance, she said, "Yes, you dunderhead."

Glad he hadn't been the one to question her—William didn't exactly know what a dunderhead was, but he didn't want to be one in her mind's eye—William straightened, his chest puffed out. "I can see to it. I know where you left them," he offered.

Mr. Smithton held up a staying hand. "Wait. Before you go off removing the baronet's property, what's this all about?"

Mrs. McNulty gave a huff. "The contest, of course."

"I understand that," the driver replied. "What's the concern?"

The housekeeper glanced around, as if to be sure no one else was about. "We cannot have anyone winning it except Mrs. Longburn," she stated.

Shrugging, the driver pretended nonchalance. "Who else would enter?"

Scoffing, she rolled her eyes. "Miss Kate? Miss Eloise? Despite her age, I wouldn't put it past Mrs. Stafford to enter," she added.

"What about Miss Barrow?" William suggested. "She's not as pretty as Mrs. Longburn, but she's certainly younger than Mrs. Stafford," he commented. "And don't the entrants have to be young enough to have children?"

"Oh, dear," the housekeeper mused. "I hadn't thought of Miss Barrows, seein' as how she seems sweet on the parson," she added.

"I thought the parson was sweet on her," Mr. Smithton remarked. "If you catch my meaning," he added, waggling his brows.

"Mr. Smithton!" the housekeeper scolded, her mouth rounding in shock. She quickly clamped it shut.

"No offense intended, Mrs. McNulty," he replied. "I'm not the only one of that opinion. They don't exactly hide their regard for one another. Which might be considered rather scandalous for a man of the cloth," he added.

Ignoring the comment, Mrs. McNulty clasped her hands together. "Now that Mrs. Longburn has moved into Wilson Hall, surely Reverend Trayfor will move into the parsonage," she said, pretending she hadn't heard the comment about the gossip surrounding the parson and the current owner of the boarding house. Apparently the two had been spotted walking hand-in-hand about the village on evening walks, their manner with one another all too familiar. Why, if the parson wasn't careful, he would be accused of having an *affaire* with Miss Barrows.

"It's none of my business, but I think he's courting her," William said, his voice kept low.

Mrs. McNulty huffed again. "Well, if he is, let's hope she doesn't enter the contest," she said. "Now, what about any girls from Torquay? Any from Livermead?"

Mr. Smithton and William exchanged glances. "Don't know any of them personally," the driver commented. "Don't think my wife does, either, other than the owner of that dress shop in Torquay."

"Madame de la Quois," William stated, carefully pronouncing each word of the name. "She's about the right age, I suspect."

"Have you made her acquaintance?" the housekeeper asked, a look of worry crossing her features for an instant.

"Don't want to," William said, his attention on Mrs. McNulty. He wanted to wink at her as a means of sending her a secret message, but he feared she would merely think he had something in his eye.

Mrs. McNulty seemed relieved at hearing his words, though. "I think one of the Baker boys is sweet on Kate," she whispered. "Which means she might not enter."

"I can't imagine Eloise entering the contest," Mr. Smithton said. "But even if she did, wouldn't Sir Adam choose Mrs. Longburn over her? If only because of Miss Penelope?"

William and Mrs. McNulty exchanged quick glances. "We can't assume anything," she said. "We must ensure Mrs. Longburn is the only one who enters the contest."

"Don't you worry your pretty head, Mrs. McNulty," William replied. "I'll be sure the flyers are removed."

The housekeeper regarded the groom a moment, her face taking on a slight blush. "That's very kind of you, Mr. Coulsden."

Mr. Smithton shook his head. "You both best be careful. If word gets out you're trying to fix the contest, there might be some angry girls after you. From Torquay," he added in a hoarse whisper.

His gaze turning on Mrs. McNulty, William said, "Don't worry, ma'am. I'll protect you," he promised.

Mrs. McNulty scoffed, but her blush was apparent when she dipped a short curtsy and said, "I'd best get back to the house."

William watched as she took her leave through the side door, his head angling to one side as he sighed loudly.

"Are you ever going to propose marriage to her?" Mr. Smithton asked as his hands went to his hips.

Tearing his gaze from the swaying hips of the housekeeper at the same moment she disappeared through the kitchen door, William frowned. "Are you ever going to retire so I can?"

The driver's brows arched up in surprise. "What are you talkin' about?"

William scoffed. "I can't exactly propose marriage whilst I'm only a *groom*," he argued.

"Oh, I think you can," Mr. Smithton countered.

"I won't."

At that moment, Sir Adam entered the stable from the same door from which Mrs. McNulty had left, his gaze darting between the groom and the driver. "Do I want to know?" he asked carefully, shaking raindrops from his greatcoat.

The two servants' eyes rounded in surprise. "Sir Adam," William said, dipping his head. "We was just talkin' about—"

"Marriage proposals," Mr. Smithton interrupted, his brows waggling.

Adam winced. "Seeing as how you're already married..." He turned his attention to the groom and raised a brow. "Am I to assume you've someone in mind to be your wife?"

William's face took on a reddish cast. "Maybe," he replied nervously. "When I'm ready. And... and she's ready," he stammered.

Adam chuckled softly. "Well, don't wait too long, Mr. Coulsden. Life can be very lonely without a bride."

Blinking, William dipped his head again. "Yes, sir." He furrowed a brow, wondering how long the baronet had been outside before he made his way into the stable. "Were you needing your horse saddled, sir?"

His attention on his Irish walker, Adam said, "I am," he replied. "But I can see to it," he added as he made his way to his horse's stall. "I'm hoping this rain lets up for a few minutes. I miss riding."

"I'll take care of it right quick for you, sir," Mr. Smithton offered before he exchanged a nervous glance with the groom.

William made his way to the hitched horses and began undoing their yokes, his gaze occasionally darting in the direction of the baronet.

How much of their conversation with Mrs. McNulty —if any— had the baronet overheard?

CHAPTER 10
AN INVITATION TO DINNER

*T*he following day, midmorning, in the old ballroom

For the second time in two days, Charlotte received an invitation to join Sir Adam and Penelope for dinner at Wilson Hall. That Penelope delivered the invitation during their morning reading time had Charlotte suspicious.

"Your Father asked you to join him for dinner again? Tonight?"

Penelope nodded happily. "And you."

"When did this happen?" The tyke had been in her presence since she had finished her breakfast in the nursery that morning.

"'Afore breakfast."

"Before breakfast," Charlotte corrected her.

"Before breakfast. He came to the nursery to see if I was awake."

"And... were you?"

Penelope grinned, her lack of bottom teeth very apparent. "I was, but I was still in my nightgown. So he tickled me, and tossed me in the air, and told me to join him for dinner at seven o'clock."

Charlotte's eyes rounded in alarm. "He tossed you in the air?"

Grinning in delight, Penelope said, "He catches me, of course. I like it, and it makes him smile."

A pang in Charlotte's chest had her giving a start. Such a simple act for Sir Adam to do to make his young daughter happy, and yet Penelope thought it important that she mention it made *him* happy as well.

"That's when he told me we are to join him for dinner at seven o'clock," Penelope added.

"Do you already know how to tell the time?" Charlotte asked, remembering how the tyke had noticed there was no number seven on her chronometer.

Her eyes darting to the side, the youngster seemed to think on the question for a moment before she said, "I know that seven o'clock is when the big hand is straight up and the little hand is pointing to the number seven."

Charlotte blinked. "How did you learn that?"

"I taught her," Sir Adam said from where he was leaning against the double-door opening at one end of the large room. Just beyond him was the flight of steps that had been used to access the fourth floor back when it had been a ballroom. The stairs at the opposite side were somewhat hidden and meant to be used by the servants. Charlotte and Penelope had used the servant stairs to access the new playroom that morning since they were closer to the nursery. "Can't have you be the only one she learns from," he added as he made his way in their direction, his boot heels clicking loud on the wooden floor.

Quickly rising to her feet and helping Penelope to do the same, Charlotte waited until Sir Adam bowed before she curtsied. Penelope followed suit, holding her skirts out to the side as she did so.

"Mrs. Longburn," Adam said as he lifted her hand. He was sure he felt a slight tremble beneath them as he brushed his lips over her knuckles, and he held onto her slender fingers a moment longer than was necessary. For some reason, it gave him a good deal of satisfaction when he heard her slight inhalation of breath.

"I'll be sure she's ready to join you for dinner at seven o'clock, sir," Charlotte said.

Adam was already seeing to his daughter's chubby fist, though, kissing it repeatedly until Penelope was giggling. He pulled her into a brief embrace and then set her back on her feet, holding her out at arm's length.

"That's a lovely gown you're wearing, Poppet. I recognize that fabric." He'd had nearly a hundred bolts of the pale pink muslin brought in from France the Season prior when he learned that modistes would be pushing the color for day gowns.

"Thank you for having it made for me, Father."

"You'll join us, too, won't you?" Adam asked as he straightened, turning his attention to Charlotte.

"Me, sir?"

Adam glanced around the large room before saying, "Yes, you. I'd like to learn what your plans are for educating my daughter." His gaze paused on the sparse furnishings set up near the room's only fireplace, their arrangement on an old Turkish carpet suggesting a parlor. In the area in which they stood were two wooden chairs, a small table, the bookshelf from Penelope's nursery, and a candle lamp. Although light flooded the room—there were several east- and west-facing windows but none on the north and south sides—he had no idea how long the large room would remain bright enough to be used as a classroom.

Overhead was a series of three large chandeliers. Each one hung from a pulley over which a decorative rope had been strung to allow them to be lowered so their candles could be lit.

In one corner was a multi-level stage built of oak and varnished to a high shine. The construct had him wondering if his forebears had hosted charades in the room until he realized a chamber orchestra would fit on the various levels during balls.

He returned his attention to his daughter. "You've the beginnings of quite a comfortable house here," he commented.

"Thank you, Father," Penelope replied, beaming in delight.

"Why, you'll no doubt be hosting balls up here before long."

Her eyes widened. "Oh, could I?" Penelope asked as she bounced on the balls of her feet.

Adam realized his mistake too late in mentioning such an event. "Uh, eventually," he replied, sobering as his gaze darted to Charlotte. "It will depend on some other matters that have come up of late."

Charlotte was sure the baronet's face was flushed, but she couldn't sort why until she remembered the upcoming village fair. "By chance, would those matters involve the Lady Wilson contest, sir?" she asked.

Giving a start, Adam blinked. "You know of it?"

Charlotte nodded. "I saw the announcement in the

mercantile yesterday." When she noticed his expression of discomfort, she added, "A rather expeditious way of finding a wife, and from what my late husband told me, it seemed to have worked quite well for your grandfather."

Adam felt the heat of embarrassment color his neck and face. "I wasn't aware of how the third baronet met and married Grandma Gertrude until just a few days ago," he murmured. "Since I haven't been home enough of late to meet any young ladies..., well, it just seemed..." He allowed the sentence to trail off before he cleared his throat.

"Expeditious," Charlotte murmured. "Which had me wondering if perhaps you might allow Miss Penelope to host the proceedings during the village fair?"

Blinking several times, Adam seemed at a loss for words.

"You'll require someone to be in charge," she reminded him. "Someone to assemble the ladies at the fair," she explained, when he didn't appear convinced. "Mrs. Stafford and Mrs. Baker are seeing to a stage, and Mr. Coulsden will provide a curtain behind which the contestants can stand until such time as they would be revealed to you and ... to everyone else."

Shifting nervously, Adam dared a glance over at his daughter before he said, "You seem to have put a good deal of thought into this," he said in a low voice.

"As have the fair organizers. I've the impression they're quite happy that this contest will replace the pie-eating contest," she added, in a hoarse whisper.

"Oh, yes," Adam murmured. "That was quite a messy affair. Berries everywhere. I seem to remember lemon, as well." He displayed a grimace for a moment.

"Those lemon pies did result in a suitable marriage for Miss Sherman," Charlotte remarked.

Adam scoffed. "I could have sworn Elijah Stafford didn't like lemon."

"Oh, he doesn't," Charlotte affirmed.

Adam attempted to suppress a chuckle, but failed. He glanced down at his daughter. "Do you suppose she's capable of hosting such an affair?" he asked. "She's not even six years old."

Charlotte furrowed a brow, surprised he would speak of his daughter as if she wasn't standing right in front of him. "You should ask her, sir."

Wincing, Adam took Penelope's hand and, with a quelling glance in Charlotte's direction, he led her to the area that had been set up as a parlor. He lifted Penelope onto the settee and then took one of the adjacent chairs.

Charlotte remained behind in the area that was

clearly the classroom, taking a seat in one of the wooden chairs and opening a book as if she didn't intend to eavesdrop on their conversation.

"So, Poppet, if you'll recall when we had tea the other afternoon with Reverend Trayfor—"

"I do," she replied. "We were discussing a wife for you."

Surprised she remembered more than having enjoyed tea and cake, Adam nodded. "Yes. And I know we haven't discussed a new mother for you in the past," he said as he leaned his elbows on his knees. "But I think it is time I find a wife."

"It is," she replied. "Because you need an heir," she added.

"Exactly," Adam agreed, rather impressed she remembered.

"He'll be my baby brother," Penelope said.

"Yes. And with time, there might be other brothers and sisters, too."

Penelope's blonde brows furrowed. "How many?" she asked, obviously suspicious.

Adam's gaze darted in Charlotte's direction, and he felt a flash of annoyance at seeing she was reading a book. Or at least, she was pretending to read. He was fairly sure she was eavesdropping. "That depends on who I take to wife and how many babies she can have," he replied.

Penelope's brows remained furrowed. "Will I still be your daughter?"

His eyes widening in shock, Adam said, "Of course, Poppet. You'll *always* be my daughter. Forever."

Her fists clutching at the pink fabric of her skirts, Penelope seemed to consider his response for a time before she said, "Will I help choose your wife?"

Adam inhaled to answer and then let out the breath. "I was thinking you might help at the contest. As the hostess." He once again glanced in Charlotte's direction, annoyed when she turned a page in the book. Apparently, she really was reading the book. "It would be sort of like a tea party, but it would be on a stage at the fair, and only ladies would be in attendance."

"And one of those ladies would become your wife?" Penelope asked.

"Exactly."

"How?"

He cleared his throat. "Well, I would have to choose one. With your help, of course."

"But what about courting her?" Penelope asked. "You have to court a woman before you ask for her hand in marriage."

Wincing, Adam wondered if it was too late to have the announcements removed from all the places Mrs.

McNulty had posted them. "I will still court the winner, of course," he replied, realizing he couldn't simply marry someone he didn't know.

"So, then why hold the contest?"

When he dared another look in Charlotte's direction, he was startled when she closed the book she had been reading and returned his gaze. The way she angled her head had him realizing she had definitely heard the last question and wondered the very same thing. "Well, as you know, I haven't been in Cockington very much of late, and I don't know all the young ladies in the village. Or in Torquay, or Livermead, or the other nearby villages, for that matter. I wouldn't know where to start with courting anyone," he explained. "This contest will allow me to learn about all the young ladies who are looking to marry," he added. "As the hostess, you can ask the contestants important questions, and their answers will help me choose one of them."

Penelope considered his response a moment before she brightened. "All right. I will be your hostess, Father," she stated. "But what if *I* don't like any of the ladies?"

Adam displayed a look of dismay. "Well, surely you would agree to at least *one* of them," he argued.

Her face screwed up in an expression of uncertainty.

"What is it?" he asked as he reached out to take one of her fists in his hand.

"Promise me you won't let your new wife send Charlotte away," Penelope said in a trembling voice. She looked as if she was on the verge of tears.

Adam's brows furrowed. "Oh, Poppet, I promise I won't let that happen," he said as he pulled her from the settee and into his arms. "She's your governess." As he held her close, his attention went back to Charlotte.

A beam of light from the nearest window cast her in a golden white glow, her red hair blazing and her pale skin translucent.

Struck by her beauty, Adam felt his entire body respond. If he hadn't been holding his daughter, he would have made his way to the widow and taken her into his arms. Would have kissed her quite thoroughly and without apology. Stripped her naked in that beam of light and kissed every square inch of her body. Demanded she do the same for him.

Where they would make love, he had no idea. There wasn't a stick of furniture in the ballroom that would accommodate her long limbs, and the old Turkish carpet was too worn for comfort.

Adam was about to imagine how she might straddle him whilst he sat in one of the wooden chairs. How he would see to it she was pleasured until she whimpered with need before riding him to a quick and satisfying release.

He suppressed the urge to groan and inhaled softly, glad his erection was hidden by the skirt of his long top coat.

Whatever did men of his grandfather's time do in similar circumstances? Their top coats had been cutaway in the front, their breeches ill equipped to hide the evidence of their erections. They would have been on display for anyone who might be watching.

They probably didn't have gorgeous, red-headed widows living in their homes seeing to their children.

"I promise I won't let that happen," he repeated before he kissed her forehead and lowered her until her feet touched the ground.

Penelope gave him a watery grin and then sobered. "I have to return to my studies now, Father."

"Oh, of course," he replied as he took a moment to straighten his top coat before he regained his feet. "I'll see you two at dinner tonight," he added as he bowed and quickly made his way across the ballroom floor and out the double-doors.

. . .

harlotte watched him go, wondering at the strange expression he had directed her way while he held his daughter. For a moment, she had thought him angry with her. In the next, she had felt naked, as if he could see through her clothes. A moment later, and her body had come alive with a myriad of sensations, her skin tingling and her heart racing, her quim dampening and her nipples hardening as he gazed at her.

Then, all at once, the spell was broken, and embarrassment had her cheeks coloring to match her hair.

It took a moment before she was settled enough to reopen the book and read it to Penelope.

CHAPTER 11
A MISCHIEVOUS MISSION

ater that afternoon

As soon as Penelope was back in the care of her nursemaid—supposedly napping—Charlotte set off for the village in the company of the groom, William Coulsden. Although she had thought to walk the half-mile to the butcher's shop, the groom had offered her a ride in the estate's small gig. "Have to fetch Mrs. McNulty's orders for the cook," he had said.

Knowing the groom held a candle for the housekeeper and would do anything for her, Charlotte grinned. "It's good of you to offer, Mr. Coulsden," she said as she stepped up and took her place on the small bench.

"Oh, I'd do anything for Mrs. McNulty," William

said before he dipped his head, as if he was embarrassed by his claim.

Charlotte gave a start, realizing the groom misunderstood her comment, but she thought better of correcting him. "If you don't think it too personal, I thought to ask you about your relationship to our employer."

William checked the rigging and hooked the reins on the pole. "Relationship?" he repeated before understanding dawned on his haggard features. He and his brother, Theodore, shared the same sagging cheeks and bald pate. "Oh, you mean because our grandmothers were sisters?"

Grinning, Charlotte said, "Yes. I wondered if you might know what was so special about your great aunt Gertrude that had Sir Winston choosing her from all the other contestants in the Lady Wilson contest?"

The older man hoisted himself onto the gig and took up the reins, chuckling as he did so. "She cheated."

Her eyes rounding in shock, Charlotte scoffed. "Mr. Coulsden," she scolded.

Ignoring her rebuke, William chuckled. "Actually, it was *my* grandmother who did the cheatin'," he clarified. "Saw an opportunity, she did. To get herself hired in Wilson Hall," he explained. "Now, don't get me wrong —there were some who knew Gertie was the best gel for the baronet, given her temperament and all. But with about, oh...” He seemed to think for a time before he said, “Twenty other gels, I think it ’twas, Aunt Gertie had some competition.”

Charlotte winced. Would there be that many young women vying for the current baronet? Or more? “So, what did your grandmother do, exactly?” she prompted.

“Gossiped, she did. Started rumors about some of the girls. Not all bad, but...” He angled his head to the side. “Enough so as to cast doubt on their suitability.”

Charlotte felt a wave of disappointment. The very last thing she wished to do to gain any advantage was gossip about any of the other contestants. “I really don’t think I could do that,” she said on a sigh.

William’s eyes widened as he glanced over at her. “Thinking to enter the contest, are you?” He couldn’t hide the sound of hope in his voice.

Shrugging as if she hadn’t given it much considera-tion, Charlotte said, “It was just a thought. You see, I made a promise to Miss Penelope’s mother that I would look after her, and it just seems marrying the baronet would ensure I could see to the girl.”

A look of understanding dawned on the groom’s face. “So, that’s why you’re her governess now, is it?” His expression brightened. “Because you’re keeping that promise?”

"Well, yes," she admitted. "That, and I really don't have anything else to keep me occupied these days," Charlotte explained.

"You'd make a right fine wife for the baronet," the groom commented. "Everyone says you already make the perfect mother for that tyke of his."

"It's very kind of you to say so," Charlotte replied, happy to learn she wasn't thought of as an opportunist by those who worked in the household.

"Wouldn't take much to see to it you didn't have anyone in the way of competition," he said, not mentioning the discussion Mrs. McNulty had started in the stable that morning. "If you're lookin' to become her mother by marriage." He slowed the gig as they approached the butcher's shop. "I know where all the flyers are posted," he said in a low voice.

Charlotte blinked. "You do?" She knew exactly where the flyers were located in Cockington, but she wasn't sure about any others outside of the village.

"Who do you think drove Mrs. McNulty all over this part of Devonshire two mornings ago?" he asked rhetorically, one of his bushy brows arched in a comical manner. He realized he might have a cohort in the crime of removing the contest flyers from windows. The thought of what he was about to do had him remembering Mrs. McNulty. It had been her suggestion they remove the flyers. By doing so, he knew it would improve her opinion of him.

"Whatever are you suggesting, Mr. Coulsden?" Charlotte asked in mock alarm.

"That we go get 'em," he said as she stepped down from the gig. "Besides, they don't have enough information on them to do anyone any good," he added.

Charlotte allowed the groom to help her down. "Enough information?"

They headed into the butcher shop. Before William was halfway into the building, he reached over and plucked the flyer from the window and handed it to Charlotte. "Nothin' here about where to apply."

"They're supposed to show up at the stage at the village fair," Charlotte countered. "At noon."

"Nothin' here about *how* to apply."

Charlotte scoffed. "They just have to be at the fair," she replied.

"Nothin' here about exactly how they should send their qualifications to the baronet."

"They just have to be unmarried and able to have children," Charlotte replied, pointing to the flyer.

"Aunt Gertie knew how to play piano-forté. Sang like a bird. But then, so did half of the other contestants," he said, ignoring Charlotte's comments.

Charlotte wasn't about to claim an ability to sing,

but she could play. "What did the others know how to do?"

He shrugged before the butcher appeared from the back of the shop. Given the time of day, his apron was bloodied, and a hunk of meat tied with string hung from a fat fist. "How do?" Mr. Fraser asked.

"I'm here for the Wilson Hall order," William announced before he turned to Charlotte and said, "Paint, draw, speak French—"

"I speak French," Charlotte murmured.

"Dance, sew, do charades—"

"Charades?" Charlotte repeated with a grimace.

"There was even an opera singer."

Charlotte's eyes widened. From the way the groom's eyebrows waggled, she knew the opera singer probably possessed other talents that had absolutely nothing to do with singing.

"You talkin' about that Lady Wilson contest?" the butcher asked as he finished wrapping the hunk of beef in a square of linen.

"We are," William replied. "Know anyone who plans to enter?" he asked as he waved a finger at the flyer Charlotte still held.

Mr. Fraser guffawed. "From *this* village?" he replied before turning his attention to Charlotte. "'Asides you, I don't know anyone who isn't already matched up, married, or too old to want a husband, exceptin' Miss Barrows over at the boarding house."

About to put voice to what she knew about Barbara Barrows, Charlotte was prevented from doing so when a familiar woman entered the shop.

"How do, Mr. Fraser?" the older woman greeted the butler. She turned to the groom and gave him an assessing glance. "Really, William, must you wear the same shirt every day?" Mrs. Coulsden asked with annoyance.

William frowned at his sister-by-marriage. "It's not the same shirt, Ellie. Got three of these, I do. They're all the same color, is all," he argued.

When the mercantile clerk's wife acknowledged her, Charlotte dipped a curtsy. "So good to see you again, Mrs. Coulsden."

"And you, Mrs. Longburn. Rumor has it you'll be running the Lady Wilson contest at the village fair."

The pleasant expression on Charlotte's face quickly changed to one of alarm. "Oh, actually Miss Penelope will be hosting the event," she replied, eager to set the record straight.

The clerk's wife waved a hand as she accepted a package from the butcher. "Well, you'll have your hands full. I expect at least a dozen young ladies will be showing up to compete for the baronet's hand," Mrs. Coulsden claimed.

"You do?" Charlotte asked, feeling as if a rock had dropped into her stomach. "That many?"

"Word's out all over town and beyond," Ellie Coulsden claimed, waving her free hand. "Wouldn't be surprised if we had contestants from the surrounding counties."

Charlotte struggled to hide her disappointment at hearing the comment. "I'll be sure Miss Penelope is prepared," she murmured.

She and the groom watched his sister-in-law take her leave of the butcher's shop before Charlotte gave him a look of disappointment. "Even if we remove all the flyers, it seems word has already spread."

"Oh, don't you worry your flaming red head about it," William said with a guffaw. "Once the flyers have been gone a few days, there'll be something else for people to talk about."

"Yeah, the lamb contest," Mr. Fraser said as he plunked a linen-wrapped package on the counter. "Tell Mrs. McNulty I'll have her lamb next week, after the fair."

"Will do," William replied as he lifted the beef from the counter.

The butcher straightened. "When are ya' gonna make an honest woman out of her?"

William blinked. "Mrs. McNulty?" he murmured, his gaze darting in Charlotte's direction as color rose in his haggard cheeks.

"Yes, Mrs. McNulty. Rumor has it you two have been carryin' on in the butler's pantry when the master is away on his trips."

His eyes rounding, William shook his head. "Ain't nothin' like that goin' on betwixt us," he claimed. "Who'd you hear that from?" he asked as he fisted one of his hands.

Mr. Fraser grinned. "Och, I was just teasin' ya, but from your reaction, now I know you're holdin' a candle for her. Right fine woman she is. You could do a whole lot worse," he claimed.

For a moment, William looked as if he was going to hurl the hunk of beef at the butcher, but he seemed to think better of it and said, "You're right. She is a right fine woman. Prob'ly too fine for me."

Scoffing, the butcher waved a hand in dismissal and disappeared through the door behind the counter.

"I'll get the door," Charlotte offered, feeling sorry for the groom.

Once they were back on the gig, Charlotte realized she still held the flyer in one hand.

"One down, three to go," the groom said with a grin, the verbal altercation with the butcher apparently forgotten.

"I already have the one from the mercantile," Charlotte admitted. When he glanced at her, a look of shock on his face, she added, "I didn't mean to take it, but I was still holding onto it yesterday when I bought embroidery threads from your brother."

William chuckled. "Well, then it's off to the bakery and then we'll head over to Livermead," he said with some excitement.

"What if someone sees me take it?" Charlotte asked with worry. She didn't want word to get back to Sir Adam that she had been seen removing the flyers.

"I'll take care of it," the groom promised. "You just see to buying us something to tide us over until dinner, and I'll just quiet-like take it. Oh, and don't forget Mrs. McNulty's order."

Charlotte nearly rolled her eyes, but the thought of treating herself to one of the meat pies that George Stephens made from recipes that had been passed down to him from his grandmother had her mouth watering. "I feel as if we're committing some sort of crime," Charlotte said in a quiet voice.

The groom guffawed. "Can't say as how stealin' flyers would have the local constable called out," he said with a grin. "And I rather doubt the news would make the news-sheet in Torquay."

Charlotte stiffened. "The news-sheet?" she repeated. "Oh, dear."

"What?"

"What if there's been an article about the contest in the Torquay newspaper?" she asked in alarm.

The query had William sobering. "Well, I'd go try collecting all of them, but I know I don't have enough blunt to buy every copy," he murmured. "But what makes you think it made the papers?"

Giving the groom a quelling glance, Charlotte said, "Mr. Baker printed the flyers. He's the one who prints the *Torquay Chronicle*," she explained. She could just imagine him filling a section of the news-sheet with information about the contest, especially if there was already an article about the village fair.

"So, you're thinking he thought it newsworthy enough to write an article about it for the paper?"

Even on a busy day in Torquay, how much news could there be? "I am," Charlotte replied with a sigh.

"Och, after five days, no one will even remember it," William replied, waving a gnarled hand as if he were swatting a fly. "The women will be going on about the vegetable contest, the ones who own sheep will be talking about the lamb contest, some comedy troupe will entertain with their juggling and bawdy jokes, and everyone else will just be happy to have a reason to leave their homes for the day."

Charlotte considered his comments. He was right. The Lady Wilson contest was but one attraction scheduled for the village fair.

As Charlotte chose two meat pies and saw to the order for Wilson Hall, William Coulsden surreptitiously removed the flyer from the bakery's small window. Stuffing it into his vest, he turned and was about to head to the gig to wait for Charlotte when Mrs. Stafford confronted him.

"What have you there?" she asked, suspicious. "Helping yourself to one of Mr. Stephens' baked goods?"

William shook his head. "I was not, Mrs. Stafford. Just... just thought I'd read this here flyer," he said as he pulled the paper from his waistcoat.

"William Coulsden," she scolded. "Everyone knows you can't read," she added as she glanced at the paper. "And you don't have any relations who could qualify to enter the Lady Wilson contest."

Caught red-handed, he leaned over and said, "I wanted to show it to Mrs. Longburn, seeing as how she's eligible to enter the contest."

Mrs. Stafford's eyes widened, as if she detected a

morsel of gossip. "Oh. Do you suppose she's interested in the baronet?" she asked in a whisper.

William straightened. "Wants to be Miss Penelope's mother, she does," he replied, nodding conspiratorially.

The older matron's mouth rounded. "She is rather good with the tyke," Mrs. Stafford remarked. "Used to be a friend of Lady Wilson, too, from what I heard. From when they lived in the capital."

His gaze darting into the bakery to check on Charlotte's progress with the meat pies, William said, "Tell me, have you heard of anyone who plans to enter the Lady Wilson contest?" he asked, deciding he may as well ask one of the fair organizers what she knew.

Mrs. Stafford furrowed her brows as she seemed to think on the query a moment. "None from around here, exceptin' Eloise or Kate or Barbara Barrows, but none of them will admit to entering," she said. "Now I haven't heard who might be eligible in Livermead," she continued. "Or in Torquay," she added as she rolled her eyes. "Surely the baronet would know better than to marry someone from there."

William wondered what it was about Torquay that seemed to have the local women eschewing the women there. "Surely," he mimicked, if only to sound agreeable.

The two turned when Charlotte emerged from the

bakery. "Good afternoon, Mrs. Stafford," Charlotte said as she approached the gig.

"Mrs. Longburn. I trust the arrangements for the bride contest are coming along nicely?"

Charlotte hesitated a moment. "The baronet has agreed to allow his daughter to act as the hostess for the contest."

Mrs. Stafford's eyes rounded. "Miss Penelope?"

Nodding, Charlotte placed her basket with the meat pies on the bench of the gig. "She's quite excited about the prospect, although she does have some concerns. The winner will be her stepmother, of course, so she has a stake in who is chosen."

The older matron seemed to think on the comment a moment before she said, "Oh, I see." She scoffed. "Still, she's so *young*. She may not know what's best for her father."

"*Who's* best," Charlotte said, wincing when she realized she was correcting an elder. "Who's best for her father, I mean."

Mrs. Stafford blinked, her brows furrowed in confusion. "Well, I really must be on my way," she said, giving Charlotte a curious glance.

"Good day," Charlotte said as she curtsied. Once the woman had disappeared into the bakery, Charlotte winced again. "Oh, I cannot believe I said that," she murmured.

"Correctin' her grammar, you mean?" William asked, his eyes twinkling as he took up the reins.

"Perhaps I'm spending too much time with my charge," Charlotte said as she handed him a meat pie.

"Thank ye," he said before taking a huge bite. When he'd swallowed most of it, he said, "I wouldn't worry about it. But have you considered that 'what's best' and 'who's best' might be the same?"

Charlotte regarded him a moment before she gave her head a slight shake. "I suppose you could be right," she murmured.

If she didn't have the impression Sir Adam disliked her—besides her history as one of Alice's friends, she had made a pest of herself what with the recommendation that the fourth floor be emptied for Penelope's use—she might simply enter the contest along with whoever else showed up and take her chances.

She was quiet for the rest of the ride to Livermead.

CHAPTER 12
PORT AND PENNIES

*L*ater that night

"Will you be having port after dinner this evening, Father?" Penelope asked from where she sat to the right of Sir Adam at the small table in the Wilson Hall dining room.

Adam smirked, remembering the day he had returned to discover his daughter was learning how to host a dinner party. "I suppose I might," he hedged, his mind on matters of silk.

"Will you be joining us ladies in the parlor after you finish your port? For a cup of tea?" she asked.

Exchanging a quick glance with Charlotte, who was failing at suppressing a grin, Adam said, "I have a better idea. How about I retire to the parlor with you?

Drink my port there?" He had spent the entire evening trying to determine the fabric of the emerald green dinner gown Charlotte wore, and he still wasn't sure if it was silk. Whatever it was, he was imagining how it would look among the other offerings in the draper shop in London.

Penelope's eyes widened, and she looked to Charlotte as if for guidance on how to respond.

"As master of the house, your father is entitled to drink his port in whatever room he would like," Charlotte said, directing her response to Penelope.

Her expression suggesting she didn't quite believe her governess, Penelope turned to her father. "If I agree, will you let me try a sip of your port?"

"Penelope," Charlotte scolded.

Adam waved a hand. "It's all right." He turned his attention on his daughter. "Not that I'm making any deals here, you understand, but I'll let you try my port," he replied. "However, if you disparage the taste, or I see you so much as wince, then I get to join you for tea in the parlor after every dinner."

Penelope screwed up her face as if she sensed a trap. "Disparage?" she repeated carefully, obviously unfamiliar with the word.

"Dislike," Adam clarified.

Blinking, Penelope seemed confused for a moment before she understood. "But what if I *want* you to join me for tea in the parlor after every dinner?" Her eyes suddenly widened and she dipped her head a moment.

Noticing how Charlotte raised her napkin to cover her smirk, Adam regarded Penelope with one of his own and sighed. "Then you only need to ask me," he replied before his expression turned to one of alarm when he saw what rested in the palm of her hand. "What's happened, Poppet?"

"It fell out," Penelope said as she grinned, her attention on one of her front teeth. "I almost swallowed it," she said, her words coming out with a distinct lisp.

"Be sure to leave it in your shoe tonight," Charlotte reminded her.

Penelope's look of concern brightened considerably as she tested her other front tooth with the tip of her tongue. "This one's loose, too," she lisped.

Grimacing, Adam glanced over at Charlotte. "Are you quite sure this is supposed to happen?"

She nodded. "There's nothing to be concerned about, sir. It's perfectly natural for children to lose their teeth."

He scoffed. "How is she supposed to eat?"

Charlotte was about to explain that the lack of front

teeth wouldn't impede his daughter's ability to eat, but thought better of it. "Well, eating apples will prove to be difficult for a few weeks," she admitted. "But she'll manage almost anything else." Charlotte turned her attention back to Penelope to see that she was now missing both of her front teeth. The girl was beaming in delight as she held her second front tooth in her other palm.

"I do hope you have a couple of pennies," Charlotte whispered, intending for her words to be heard only by Adam.

"And if I don't?" Adam asked, pretending happiness at seeing his daughter's teeth.

"I might. I'll have to check my reticule."

"This is all your fault," Adam said in a hoarse whisper.

Charlotte blinked before she turned to stare at him. "How is this my fault?"

"You read her that little mouse book."

"I did no such thing," she countered. "I don't even own that book, and neither do you." She was about to continue defending herself when she noticed his smirk had returned. "What is it?"

Adam chuckled. "You. It isn't hard to unnerve you, is it?" he teased. "You're nearly as red as your hair."

Huffing, she crossed her arms, which had his gaze darting to her suddenly apparent cleavage. Although he attempted to hide his interest by quickly glancing over at his daughter, Adam knew he'd been caught when Charlotte inhaled sharply and dropped her arms.

"Sir Adam," she scolded quietly.

"Father," Penelope chimed in, the word not coming out quite right given her lack of front teeth.

"Forgive me," he said before clearing his throat. "Why don't you two head to the parlor, and I'll just—"

"Join us when you've finished your port," Charlotte interrupted, determined he not change what they had previously discussed.

"I've a better idea," he countered suddenly. He turned to Penelope. "Take your teeth upstairs and put them in your Sunday best slippers," he instructed. "Change into your nightgown, put on a dressing gown, and then come to my study for some port." He gave her a wink.

A toothless grin appeared. "Yes, Father," Penelope said with excitement as Adam stood and helped her down from her chair. She hurried out of the dining room.

Sensing the invitation to the study would allow him some alone time with his daughter, Charlotte pushed back from the table. "I'll retire to my apartments now, sir."

"You will not," he said, alarmed by her comment. "You're coming to the study, too. It's warmer there than in the parlor."

Charlotte blinked. "I am?"

His determination faltered somewhat. "Won't you?" His head dipped a moment before he raised it so his chin was more apparent.

Unsure of his motive for the change in venue, Charlotte said, "All right. Should I have Harris bring the tea tray there?"

"If you insist," Adam replied. "Or... you can join me in a port or... or a brandy."

The thought of trying a glass of brandy—she'd only tried a single sip in the past—had Charlotte curious. "Are you really going to allow Penelope to drink spirits?" she asked, an expression of worry on her face.

Adam sighed. "I am. She'll take one sip and announce that it's the worst drink she's ever tasted, and that will be the end of it."

Charlotte blinked. "How can you be so sure?"

"Isn't that how *you* reacted the first time you tried port?" he countered.

Her eyes darting to the side, Charlotte said, "I actually enjoy the taste of port, sir."

Adam blinked. "Oh." He seemed at a loss for a moment. "Well, this is a surprise. What is your opinion of brandy?"

Giving him a quelling glance, Charlotte said, "I've only had it the one time. I must admit a preference for port."

"Hmph," he responded. "Interesting."

"Interesting?" she repeated.

He grinned and then offered his arm. "You are an enigma, Mrs. Longburn," he stated. "The next thing you'll be telling me is that you intend to enter the Lady Wilson contest."

Charlotte's eyes rounded. Had the baronet learned she wanted to be Penelope's mother? But she saw mischief in his eyes, and she relaxed. "Are you *expecting* me to enter the contest, Sir Adam?"

Adam inhaled as if to answer and then seemed to reconsider his response. "You think it ridiculous, don't you? The contest, I mean?"

Shaking her head, Charlotte placed an arm on his and said, "Not at all. It worked well for Sir Winston. There's no reason to think it won't work for you."

The baronet seemed lost in thought for a moment before he announced, "I'm thinking of cancelling the contest," as they headed out of the dining room and through the hall toward the study.

Charlotte nearly stumbled. "But... but you can't. Mrs. Stafford said there will be over a dozen young ladies from all over Devonshire in attendance." At his look of alarm, she added, "Although..."

Adam paused to allow her to enter the study before him. "Although?" he prompted.

"She seems to think a young woman from Torquay wouldn't make for a suitable match."

Furrowing a brow, Adam asked, "Did she say why?"

Charlotte shared his questioning look. "No, but she wasn't the only one who made such a comment. I believe Mrs. Baker was of the same opinion."

"Hmph. Good to know," Adam replied as he led her to a chair near the fireplace.

Charlotte took a seat in a plush upholstered wing-back chair and watched as Adam moved to a credenza behind his desk. He poured two glasses of port from a crystal decanter and offered her one of them. He touched the rim of his glass to hers and said, "To your health."

"And to yours," Charlotte said before she took a sip of the tawny port. She closed her eyes and inhaled the scent of the dark liquid before she pulled the glass from her lips. When she glanced up, she discovered Adam was staring at her. "What is it?"

He gave a start. "Nothing. I...I was just reminded of something," he murmured as he took a seat in the opposite chair. "Someone," he added before he sipped his port. "Tell me, Mrs. Longburn. How long did you know Alice? Before I married her?"

Charlotte's grip on her glass tightened. The entire time she had known the baronet, he had never indicated he even knew she was a friend of Alice Winthrop. "We met when we were very young, but we became close when we were in finishing school. In London," she replied. "My father was teaching at the boys' school a few streets away."

"I knew her at least that long," he said, his brows furrowing. "Our families were quite close. I recall meeting you, of course, but I don't remember you spending an inordinate amount of time in her company."

Feeling the heat of embarrassment rising to color her neck and cheeks, Charlotte stared into her glass of port a moment before she said, "I don't believe you were aware of anyone but her."

Adam blinked. "Are you saying I was blind to everyone but my Alice?"

Charlotte angled her head to one side as she gave a one-shouldered shrug. "Love is blind, sir. Or rather makes one blind to all others. At least, that's what my father used to tell me."

His brows furrowed, Adam absently sipped his port. "As I recall, all the other girls in Alice's class at the finishing school were betrothed, most before their first Season was complete."

"That is true," Charlotte acknowledged, tempted to swallow the rest of her port in one gulp.

"And was it true for you?"

Inhaling softly, she nodded. "I was betrothed as well. However, my Federick died of cholera a few weeks after my mother succumbed to it."

Adam's eyes rounded as a long-forgotten memory emerged. "You were going to marry Frederick Turner," he murmured, his gaze turning inward. "Of Turner Textiles."

"I was."

"God, I'm so sorry for your loss. Your losses," he corrected. "Freddie was one of the good ones, too. We talked about doing business together," he murmured. "As I recall, his father had a textile mill. In Reading, I think it was."

"Yes, he did," Charlotte acknowledged, rather touched he would share his condolences after so much time had passed. "Their father retired a few years ago, so Freddie's younger brother, Benjamin, is seeing to the business now. They weave silks, mostly for livery." She reached down and pinched together some of the fabric of her dinner gown's emerald skirt. "This gown was made from one of their bolts. I know it's terribly out of fashion, but I can't bear to pass it on to a maid just yet," she said.

"I didn't know," Adam whispered. "I'm always on the lookout for new fabric sources," he added. "For my draper shop in London."

Charlotte regarded him with a curious expression. "I can give you Mr. Turner's address in Reading, if you'd like," she offered.

"You keep in touch?" he asked, his expression showing surprise.

"Not so much of late. Not since... not since I wed the parson."

"Would you have married Benjamin? If he offered?" Adam asked.

Charlotte stared at Adam, her mouth dropping open in shock at the rather bold query. "I rather doubt it. He never showed any interest in me."

"Even after his brother died?" he asked in disbelief.

Scoffing, Charlotte said, "The fact that he never showed any interest in me was probably because he's at least five years my junior and at least ten years from any interest in the parson's mousetrap."

"Oh," Adam replied, amused by her response. "Hmph."

Feeling emboldened, Charlotte asked, "Why did you bring Alice here to Cockington? After you wed?"

Adam stared at her a moment before his gaze dropped to his glass. "Father died the year before I wed, and I'd been away too long. There are people here who relied on him. People who rely on me," he corrected, thinking of the tenant farmers who worked his land. "I have a man of business who sees to the shop in London, so my presence there isn't required but a couple of times a year," he explained. He set his glass of port on a side table. "Tell me, Mrs. Longburn, why did *you* come to Cockington?"

Although she half-expected he would ask the question, Charlotte was still unprepared for how much to admit. "My father retired from teaching at the boy's school in London. He knew I missed Alice, and with the village in need of a parson, he talked Ambrose Longburn into applying for the position. Mr. Longburn spent his youth here in Cockington, you see," she explained. "The three of us moved here a month later."

"Were you betrothed to the parson when you moved here?" Adam asked, managing to hide a grimace at learning the parson had been an acquaintance in London.

Charlotte's eyes rounded. "Oh, heavens, no. I was still mourning the loss of Freddie," she replied. Feeling the effects of the port, she added, "I only married Ambrose because my father insisted on it. Said he would be dying soon, and he wanted to see me wed before that happened," she explained. "For protection, he claimed," she added quietly.

"Good of you to please your father," Adam murmured. "God knows I didn't do enough of that with my own."

Surprised at his words, Charlotte was about to ask what he meant when he drained his port. He gave the empty glass a second glance when Charlotte gasped. "What's wrong?" he asked.

"You were going to allow Penelope to try your port," she reminded him. Even as she made the comment, she could hear the girl descending the stairs.

"I can always pour more," he said as he winked. "Remember what I said. She'll make a face. I'm sure of it."

He stood when his daughter appeared on the threshold wearing a dressing gown tied at the waist, the bottom ruffle of her nightgown peeking out beneath its hem. Below that were soft slippers lined with sheepskin. Two braids of blonde hair stuck out from the sides of her head, both secured with blue ribbons. "There you are," he said as he approached her. He leaned over and took her hand to kiss the back of it.

She curtsied and then her gaze went to his empty glass. "You drank your port without me?" she asked, her expression of disappointment suggesting she might start shedding tears.

"I was just about to put the port into it," he countered. "Come. Let's get you seated by the fire. I shouldn't want you getting a chill."

"Why, that's a rather beautiful dressing gown," Charlotte said as she admired the sky blue robe Penelope wore.

"Thank you. My father had Madame de la Quois make it for me," Penelope said as she scrambled onto the chair Adam had been using.

"From one of the fabrics from his shop, no doubt," Charlotte commented.

"It was. Turns out, sky blue velvet wasn't very popular last year for winter gowns," Adam remarked as he poured more port into his glass. "I'm quite sure the madam can make you a dressing gown, as well. There's probably enough fabric left to make ten of them," he groused.

"We could have matching dressing gowns," Penelope whispered.

Charlotte grinned at the girl as Adam leaned down and offered her the glass of port.

"One sip, Poppet," he said as he lowered himself into an adjacent chair.

"Only one?" she countered before she lifted the glass to her lips and took a sip. Her gaze met Charlotte's, as if she was having second thoughts.

Charlotte raised her glass, took a matching sip, and lowered the glass before Penelope had a chance to pull her glass from her lips. When she did, she grinned, and her lack of front teeth had Charlotte doing her best to suppress a chuckle.

"Well?" Adam asked, his attention on his daughter.

"It's not my favorite," she replied, managing to keep an impassive expression. "I'd rather drink tea."

Adam exchanged a quick glance with Charlotte. "Well. I'm almost tempted to have her try brandy."

"Sir!" Charlotte scolded.

"Almost tempted," he repeated with a grin. "Come, Poppet. Let's get you up to bed," he said as he lifted her into his arms.

"You'll want to get a good night's sleep before you check your slippers in the morning," Charlotte said, her comment meant more as a reminder for the baronet than for Penelope. "Did you put your teeth in your shoe?"

Penelope nodded. "One in each Sunday slipper,"

she affirmed. "Just to see if I get two pennies," she said as she held up two fingers.

Adam chuckled. "If you put them both in the same slipper, you might have found more than two pennies," he teased. He shot a look of panic in Charlotte's direction before he carried Penelope out of the study.

Charlotte giggled, realizing she had best find some money to help out the baronet. Perhaps he had intended to leave a larger coin for the teeth because he didn't have any smaller coins in his purse.

She waited a few minutes, enjoying the port and the familiar scent that seemed to surround Adam Wilson.

When her glass was empty, she placed it on the salver and made her way up the stairs, intending to go to her apartments. Adam met her as he descended the stairs from the nursery, though, and stopped on the landing. He looked stricken, and Charlotte paused in her climb.

"Is something wrong?"

"I don't have any pennies," he whispered hoarsely.

Suppressing the urge to chuckle at his expense, Charlotte resumed her climb. "I think I have some in my reticule," she said. "You do know which slippers they're in?"

"She showed me, thank the gods," he replied as he

turned and walked beside her. "How many pairs of slippers do most young misses own these days?"

Charlotte couldn't help the bubble of laughter that erupted just then. "Surely you should know. Aren't you the one who bought them for her?"

"That's not the point," he replied defensively, definitely not sharing in her good humor.

When they reached Charlotte's apartments, she opened the door and quickly moved through the sitting area to her dressing table, half-expecting the baronet to follow. Instead, Adam remained in the corridor, nervously glancing about as if he feared being seen.

"You're welcome to wait in here," she said as she opened her reticule.

The baronet poked his head past the threshold and glanced in. "Are you quite sure?"

"Of course," she replied as she pulled her coin purse from her reticule. "How much do you want to leave in place of the teeth?" She found several pennies at the bottom and pulled them out.

"You left a penny for her two bottom teeth?" he asked.

"I did." Charlotte held out two coins.

"Well, I certainly don't want to raise her expectations too quickly," he murmured as he accepted the offering. "Now I'll owe you three."

"Four, actually," Charlotte countered.

He blinked. "You gave her a penny for *each* of her two bottom teeth?"

"I did, sir. Harris should have given them to you."

A pained expression crossed Adam's face. "I think he may have tried, and I didn't understand what he was talking about," he admitted. "Thank you for seeing to this."

"You're welcome, sir. Oh, and you might wish to keep some pennies on hand. She'll be losing more over the next year or so."

"More?" he asked in disbelief. "I could go broke buying her teeth," he complained in mock dismay.

"You'll more likely go broke buying her more slippers," Charlotte said with a grin. She inhaled softly when she realized she may have sounded too familiar with the baronet. "My apologies. It's not my place to comment on such things."

Adam furrowed a brow. "Perhaps not, but I probably need to be reminded I'm spoiling her rotten," he murmured. He glanced about, suddenly nervous. "I take it you are all moved in now?"

Charlotte nodded. "I am, sir. Thank you again for the accommodations. For the position. I'm sure the new parson appreciates having his own house now."

His brows still furrowed, Adam said, "I rather doubt that."

Blinking, Charlotte said, "Pardon, sir?"

Not about to explain what he knew regarding the parson's living arrangements, Adam said, "Never mind. I'd best be delivering these pennies now." He bowed and backed out of the apartment, leaving Charlotte wondering about Reverend Trayfor.

CHAPTER 13
A BARONET'S MORNING

The following day

A blinding light woke Adam from a restless sleep, and for a moment, he thought he had a hangover.

"Apologies, sir," Harris said as he quickly closed the drapes in the master suite.

"What *was* that?" Adam asked as he sat up and rubbed an eye with the back of his hand.

"The sun, sir." The droll delivery hid the fact that Harris was almost grinning at his master's expense.

"Finally," Adam said as he stepped out of bed and made his way to his bathing chamber. "I was beginning to think we were going to have to build an ark."

The rain that had fallen for four days straight had

moved on, leaving behind blue skies, a soaked garden, and muddy roads.

"You asked that I remind you of your meeting with the parson," Harris said as he pulled various garments from drawers and the wardrobe.

"Do I have time for breakfast?"

"I believe so, sir."

"I suppose our newest household member has already had hers," Adam said as he applied shaving soap to his face. He didn't mean to sound grumpy as he put voice to the comment, but he couldn't help it.

He was grumpy on this morning.

Harris paused in his duties. "She's having her breakfast in the nursery with Miss Penelope, sir."

About to begin shaving, Adam held the straight razor against his cheek and froze. "Did she have breakfast with Penelope yesterday morning?"

"She did, sir."

"Hmph." Adam scraped the blade over his dark beard, wondering why he was annoyed by the thought that the governess was eating with his daughter. If she didn't choose to take her meals with Penelope, then she would be left eating alone.

Penelope would be eating alone.

He almost always ate alone.

Usually he didn't mind, since he used the time to review contracts or read a book, write correspondence or read letters or the *Torquay Chronicle*.

"Tell me, Harris. Would it be so bad if I insisted my daughter join me for dinners every night?" He guided the razor over his jaw and down his neck.

"Bad, sir?" Harris replied as he appeared on the threshold of the bathing chamber. He moved to the tub and manipulated the valves for the hot water heater before turning the knobs at the bathtub. A gush of water shot into the tub as the maze of pipes moaned, groaned, and clanked. "I hardly think dining with your daughter could be considered bad, sir."

"Tell me, Harris. How old was I when I was allowed to eat in the dining room?" Adam asked. He smoothed a hand over his jaw as he peered at his reflection in the mirror.

"You ate with your parents every Sunday in the dining room until you left for Eton."

Adam paused in a mid-stroke of the razor as he tried to remember his days as a youth at Wilson Hall. He could recall dinners at Eton. He could recall meals in the Wilson townhouse in London. But for some reason, he couldn't recall eating with his parents in Wilson Hall.

"I should like my daughter to dine with me every night," he announced.

"Very good, sir," Harris replied as he tested the bath water. He winced.

"Cold or hot?" Adam asked, noticing the butler's reaction in the mirror.

"Tepid, sir."

Adam gave him a quelling glance and stepped into the tub. "Better than ice cold," he said as he lowered himself into the barely warm water. Given his tumescence that morning—he clearly remembered the dream he'd had prior to waking—he was glad for the cooler water.

For the third day in a row, he had awakened having dreamt about Charlotte Longburn. Had she been fully clothed and wearing one of her ridiculous hats, he was quite sure he wouldn't have started his days in a state of frustration. However, she had been naked. In his bed. Her long red hair loose and trailing down the front of his body as she used her long fingers to tease him into a state of sexual readiness that had him looking forward to what would come next. And then...

And then reality entered his bedchamber by way of Harris.

How dare the servant interrupt his one opportunity to enjoy a morning tumble.

Adam was almost ready to dismiss the butler.

Reason prevailed, though.

Wilson Hall would be lost without the butler that had served Adam's father as well as him since he'd inherited the baronetcy.

As for Mrs. Longburn, he had to quit dreaming of the parson's widow. She was Penelope's governess now. She held a paid position in his household. In less than a week, he would be choosing a new Lady Wilson from the contestants at the village fair. A Lady Wilson he hoped he might come to care for as much as he had Alice. A Lady Wilson who would see to an heir and perhaps a spare before she headed to London with the excuse she couldn't abide life in Cockington any longer.

He gave his head a shake. Why did he think every young woman wanted to end up in London? Was Cockington really so bad? Yes, it was small. But the villagers were a good sort. They worked hard. The local fishermen always seemed to do well. The land produced enough in the way of crops to sustain most of the baronetcy while his draper shop in London saw to paying his way in life.

He didn't mind living in London for part of the Season, but he certainly wouldn't do it if he didn't think it necessary to check on the draper shop. Meet with the brokers at Wellingham Imports. Speak with modistes about the latest French fashions.

After a few weeks, though, he was ready to return to Wilson Hall. Ready to throw his daughter into the air to hear her infectious giggles. Sleep in his own bed.

"Sir?"

Adam gave a start. "Yes, Harris?"

"Your fingers are wrinkling, sir."

Blinking, Adam held a hand up before his face and groaned. Where had the time gone? He lifted himself from the cold water and accepted the bath linen Harris offered. "Have you ordered the coach?"

"I have, sir. Mr. Smithton will be ready to leave whenever you are."

"Very good. I'll eat quickly," he said.

"Your meeting with the parson isn't for another two hours, sir," Harris commented.

"Hmph. Perhaps I'll pay a call on one of my relatives," he murmured as he slipped into the pantaloons Harris offered. "Do you suppose Mr. Coulsden is at the mercantile today?"

Harris held a waistcoat open. "If he is not, then he has died, sir," he said drolly.

"Harris," Adam scolded as he buttoned up the waistcoat. When the butler didn't apologize, Adam realized the servant had only stated the obvious. "I wish to speak with him about the last Lady Wilson contest," he murmured.

Holding out his top coat, the butler gave him a curious look. "Your groom was also present for the last contest, sir," he commented.

Adam regarded the butler a moment. "I didn't know that."

"They are brothers, which makes them both your distant cousins, sir."

"Hmph," Adam said as he pulled on his topcoat. He supposed he might have known it at one time. Back when discussions about the family had occurred at the dining table. "Do you suppose the groom was hired because he was related to Grandma Gertrude?"

"Undoubtedly," Harris replied. "As a stable boy, actually."

Adam furrowed a brow. "Were others in the family also employed as a result of the marriage?"

With a rolled cravat in one hand, Harris practically rocked on the balls of his feet when he said, "Mr. Coulsden's father and his mother." When his master was ready, Harris unrolled the cravat by holding on to one end of the white silk and allowing the rest to fall from his hand. Once it was unfurled, he wrapped it several times around Adam's neck.

From the way in which Harris made the comment,

Adam sensed the butler had more to say on the topic. "Go on," he prompted.

Harris finished tying the knot on Adam's cravat and stepped back. "After you mentioned the contest the other day, I had occasion to ask Mrs. McNulty what she remembered about it," he admitted. "From what she said about the increase in staff numbers after Sir Winston wed Gertrude Amherst, I have reason to believe there might have been some underhanded tactics employed, sir."

Adam blinked. "Underhanded tactics?" he repeated. "You mean... Grandma Gertie cheated?"

Harris winced. "Something like that, sir."

Guffawing, Adam moved to the door. Even if Gertrude Amherst had cheated to become Sir Winston's wife, she had been a welcome addition to Wilson Hall. Her ebullient nature had always delighted the household. She never put on airs nor used her title to demean others. When she died, Adam had been away at Eton. He mourned the old matron, knowing Wilson Hall would never be the same. "If it's true she cheated, well, good on her," he said before leaving his bedchamber.

From somewhere down the corridor, Harris heard Adam add, "She was the best thing that ever happened to Wilson Hall."

Harris stared after his master for several seconds

before he resumed his duties, wondering when Sir Adam would amend his assessment.

The best things that had happened to Wilson Hall since his tenure had begun were currently in the nursery.

Both of them.

CHAPTER 14
TEA WITH THE PARSON

bout two hours later

Despite the muddy roads, Mr. Smithton delivered Adam to Miss Barrows' boarding house well before his appointment with Reverend Trayfor was scheduled to begin.

"Apologies. I know I'm early," Adam said as he shook Michael Trayfor's hand in the vestibule. "It's good to see you again."

"And you," Michael replied as he indicated an upholstered chair in the parlor. "When I saw you a few days ago, I meant to ask about your latest trip. For business, was it not? I learned of it from one of your servants who manages to attend Sunday services," he added with a teasing smirk.

Ignoring the comment about him not attending

church, Adam took a seat and said, "I was in Darlington on business."

"It went well, I trust?" Michael asked as he took an adjacent chair, its upholstery worn and the floral pattern faded.

"It did. I know you probably don't care about Merino wool, but I was determined to arrange a source for it for the shop in London," Adam explained. "Contracts are all signed now. With any luck, they'll be delivered to Banks Textiles by post sometime this week."

Michael snorted. "I never could understand your fascination with fibers when we were at university," he commented. "We have excellent sheep here in Devonshire. Darlington seems a long way to go for wool. Isn't that up in Yorkshire?"

Adam nodded. "It is, but worth it, I think."

"At least now it seems you've the time for matters closer to home," Michael hinted.

Angling his head to one side, Adam gave the parson a questioning glance. "Matters?"

Michael rolled his eyes. "The Lady Wilson contest? Everyone in the village is talking about it. I think some bets have even been placed as to which young lady will be taking home the prize."

"Oh, good God," Adam replied, before his eyes suddenly widened. "Oh, pardon the curse."

The parson grinned before he chuckled. "When we last spoke, I didn't think you were really going to run a contest to find a wife," he said.

"You practically dared me to," Adam countered. "I used that old advertisement of my grandfather's to have Robert Baker print some new flyers over at the print shop in Torquay."

"Still, I didn't think you would actually go through with it," the parson commented, his grin nearly ear to ear.

Adam winced. "I was feeling a bit overwhelmed that day, I think."

Michael regarded him a moment before the boarding house's proprietress appeared on the threshold carrying a tea tray. "Oh, you sweetheart," he commented as he stood.

Adam's gaze darted to the woman before he turned it back on the parson and then belatedly stood. "Mrs. Barrows' niece, are you not?" he asked, wondering at the parson's endearment. His eyes widened when Michael gave the woman a peck on the cheek as she set the tray on the low table.

"Mr. Trayfor," she scolded. "We have a guest."

Turning to the baronet, she said, "Good morning, Sir Adam. I am Barbara. How do you take your tea?"

"Just like that," he replied as he watched her quickly pour two cups. She curtsied before hurrying out of the parlor, her face red with embarrassment.

Adam turned his attention on the parson, his mouth open in shock. "Are you always so free with your affections for one who brings tea?" he asked in a hoarse whisper.

"I think a man is entitled to kiss his *wife* on the cheek," Michael claimed as he settled back into his chair. He displayed a mischievous grin.

"Your *wife*?" Adam repeated. He glanced back in the direction in which the boarding house owner had disappeared. "Since when?"

Michael shrugged. "Since the year after we finished at university?" he replied before he chuckled. "Cockington is the first place we've been able to live together since the parish before last. I thought for certain I would get the parish here four or five years ago, but when Longburn ended up with the position..." He shrugged. "He had seniority. In the meantime, Barbara inherited the boarding house from an old aunt and moved here whilst I saw to my last flock."

Adam blinked, wondering how he hadn't known his friend was married. "She couldn't stay with you in

Cornwall?" he asked as he lifted the cup of tea Barbara had poured for him.

Michael winced. "The parsonage was a two-room shack with a leaky roof. Most of the villagers were coal miners. I couldn't do that to her."

Scoffing, Adam considered the wave of excitement that had gripped the village when Miss Barrows had reopened Cockington's only boarding house. "We all thought she was a spinster when she arrived," Adam said. "And why does everyone call her Miss Barrows?" he questioned. "Why not Mrs. Trayfor?"

Michael allowed a shrug. "If you'll recall, her aunt was Mrs. Barrows, and 'Barrow's' is what's painted on the shingle," he reminded him. "When Barbara introduced herself as Mrs. Barrow's niece, everyone assumed she was unmarried. If the old biddies don't have the good sense to learn her real name..." He shrugged.

"But you'd have those in Cockington believe you're carrying on an illicit *affaire* with her? Because... that's what they're thinking," Adam remarked, rather alarmed by his friend's cavalier attitude.

Michael chuckled. "I know. So scandalous," he teased. "Made more so now because it seems you've hired Mrs. Longburn, and she's up and moved out of the parsonage, and now everyone expects me to move into it."

Adam huffed. "And here I thought I was doing you a favor. Giving you a suitable place to live," he reasoned.

"Oh, it's fine. Really. Barbara and I will move into the parsonage after the village fair is over. Keep the two servants that have been employed there," Michael explained. "Barbara's thinking of selling the boarding house. Although it's a good living, it is a lot of work, and, well, it's time we have a child or two." He paused, noting Adam's look of expectation before he added, "Oh, all right. I'll announce the fact that I'm a married man at the next church service. Work it into the Easter sermon somehow and see how many are awake enough to sort it," he said with an exaggerated sigh.

Chuckling, Adam remembered why it was he had liked Michael Trayfor whilst they were at Cambridge. The man had a sense of humor despite his calling as an Anglican priest.

"You think me foolish, running this contest?" Adam asked as he grimaced.

Michael allowed another shrug before he lifted a plate of biscuits from the tea tray and offered it to Adam. "Actually, it's a rather novel way in which to ensure more attendance at the village fair. I hear last year's fair attendance was rather lackluster."

"The pie eating contest wasn't the draw we expected it might be," Adam reasoned. "Although there was a marriage out of it."

"Barbara felt bad for those who worked so hard to line up the vendors and such." Michael paused to take a bite of a biscuit. "Tell me. Who will you choose to be Lady Wilson?"

Adam's eyes rounded. "I have absolutely no idea. I don't even know who is entering," he claimed. "Seems I should have asked for the young ladies to send their qualifications in advance."

The parson regarded him a moment before he said, "May I ask why it is you haven't simply courted Mrs. Longburn? She's out of mourning now. She's the perfect age. She's pleasant to look upon. Miss Penelope loves her. She'd make an excellent wife."

Stiffening in more ways than one, Adam dipped his head and groaned.

"Oh, dear," Michael murmured. "I know there's some history there, what with your late wife and all. Too hard to compete with a best friend's attentions?" he gently teased.

Adam's head lifted so quickly, Michael straightened in his chair. "That was just a guess, but it seems I've hit a nerve," he said as his eyes rounded. "Out with it. Confession is good for the soul."

Moaning, Adam regarded the parson with an expression that suggested he might haul off and hit the man. "Yes, she was a friend of Alice's. Seems they knew each other from finishing school in London."

Not exactly what he was expecting to hear, Michael finished his biscuit and helped himself to another. "Is that a problem?"

Adam winced. "As I recall, Miss Wentworth—Mrs. Longburn—tried to talk my Alice out of accepting my suit."

"Because she wanted you for herself?" Michael guessed, his brow still arched in a tease.

"No!" Adam replied with indignation, although he blinked several times, as if he hadn't given that possibility a thought. "But I've actually no idea why," he whispered.

Michael scoffed. "Well, now that she's in your employ, you might broach the subject. Ask her why. Clear the air between the two of you."

"Why should I?"

Frowning, Michael was about to scold his friend but decided a different tact was necessary. "You'll never know otherwise," the parson reasoned. "For the rest of your life, you will never know."

Adam gave him a look of annoyance. "It doesn't really matter now. Alice died after giving birth, and that's the end of it."

Michael furrowed a dark brow, but decided to drop the subject. "How is Miss Penelope?"

Adam leaned back in the chair and let out a breath. "Good, I think, except she keeps losing teeth," he remarked. "Turns out it costs money when they do," he warned.

Chuckling, Michael helped himself to another biscuit. "A penny here and there won't break you," he said. "What has Mrs. Longburn been teaching her?"

Angling his head to one side, Adam shrugged. "Poppet's been learning how to read, and how to host tea parties and dinner parties and such." His brows rose with this last comment.

His eyes widening, as if he were impressed with the news, Michael said, "Mrs. Longburn seems to have been a good influence for her. I was happy to hear you hired her. She needed a distraction, and your daughter is it."

Adam straightened. "A distraction?"

Michael nodded. "Poor woman was probably bored to tears married to my predecessor. He was almost old enough to be her grandfather—"

"So why did she marry him?" Adam shot back.

Recoiling, Michael stared at his guest a moment before he said, "Like most of her sex, she had no choice."

"And why did she come to Cockington?" Adam asked, ignoring the comment. "She wasn't married to Longburn when she arrived."

Michael's brows drew together a moment as he regarded his friend. "As I understand it, she came with her father," he replied, curious as to why Adam's good mood had suddenly soured. "Mr. Wentworth was still her protector, given she wasn't yet married. Longburn and Wentworth were good friends. Longburn landed the position, and they relocated. It's as simple as that," he explained.

"Is it?" Adam asked in annoyance. "I can't help but think there was more to it," he groused as he plucked a Dutch biscuit from the salver. He stared at it a moment before he took a nibble. Finding it surprisingly good, he finished it off in another two bites. "The timing was damned curious," he added.

There was a pause before Michael asked, "Why?" He sat back and regarded his guest with an expression of bemusement.

"Because I had just returned to Cockington after living in London for Penelope's first two years. A couple of months later, and they show up."

"Could be a coincidence," Michael murmured, but like Adam, he sensed there was more to the Wentworth's move to Cockington.

Adam gave him a quelling glance. "In all the possible places in all of England, do you really think it a coincidence the Wentworths ended up here? With Longburn?"

Although he, too, was curious as to why a seasoned parson would choose to spend his last years in Cockington, Michael had never discovered the reason. "You could ask her," he urged, his voice quiet.

Adam growled.

Amused by his friend's reaction, Michael chuckled. "What's really going on here? I've never seen you like this," he claimed.

Wincing, Adam said, "The damned woman has upended my life at Wilson Hall. The entire top floor of the house had to be cleaned out in order to make way for a playroom and a classroom for Penelope." He huffed. "All the stuff that was up there came down, which is how I discovered my grandfather's papers. Which is how this infernal contest got started."

Despite the anger that sounded in his friend's words, Michael once again chuckled. "Sounds like a perfect arrangement for your daughter," he remarked. "But… that isn't all of it, is it?"

His brows furrowing, as if he suspected a trap, Adam asked, "What do you mean?"

"She's gotten under your skin."

Adam's eyes rounded. "She has not." When the parson looked as if he was going to laugh, Adam pinched his lips together before he added, "I wake up every morning having dreamt about her, dammit."

Michael sobered, his teacup halfway to his lips. He set the cup back on its saucer. "Do you… reach for her? In your bed?" When Adam didn't reply, he added, "Happens to me all the time. I dream of Barbara. Difference is, I reach out, and she's there," he murmured. "Mornings are my favorite time of the day, and it's not because of breakfast," he said, waggling his eyebrows.

"Bastard," Adam murmured. He swallowed. "Used to be, I dreamt of Alice. For years after she died, I still woke up thinking of her. Now..." He cleared his throat, feeling guilty that his morning thoughts were no longer of Alice but of Charlotte Longburn.

There were times he had difficulty conjuring Alice's image in his mind's eye. He regretted that he had but one miniature painted of her. The full-size portrait he had intended to have painted was scheduled to be done after the birth of Penelope. "One of the boxes that came down from the fourth floor has Alice's name on it," he said in a quiet voice.

"Have you opened it?"

Adam shook his head. "Not yet. I've been a bit of a coward," he admitted. "I'm almost afraid of what I'll find. But if I do, maybe I'll wake up thinking of her again," he added before he sighed in frustration.

"You should be waking up to the fact that you need a wife," Michael stated, hoping his friend's moment of melancholy had passed.

"I do. I know that. I need an heir. And in a few days, I'll choose a wife at the village fair."

Michael rolled his eyes. "Well, whatever you do, don't go choosing some chit from Torquay."

Adam's mouth dropped open. "I've already been warned about them," he replied, before helping himself to the last biscuit.

Whatever was it about young ladies from Torquay that had everyone warning him against them?

CHAPTER 15
A TIFF IN TORQUAY MAKES
THE PAPER

few minutes later, Cockington Mercantile Theodore Coulsden looked up from that day's *Torquay Chronicle* to see Sir Adam entering the shop. Although the baronet appeared preoccupied, the clerk was sure the man had a reason other than shopping for being there.

"Good morning, Sir Adam," Theodore called out.

"Cousin Ted," Adam acknowledged with a nod.

The greeting had the clerk giving a start. "I often wondered if you even knew we were related," he commented, holding out his right hand. Adam shook it.

"I probably knew when I was much younger," Adam replied, "but having spent some time going through a box of my grandfather's papers has reminded me there are a number of people here in Cockington that are relations by way of my Grandmother Gertrude," he explained.

"She was my Aunt Gertie," Theodore admitted. "And there wasn't another woman in all of England who was like her."

Chuckling, Adam said, "You have that right." He paused as he glanced around to be sure no one else was in the shop. "I wondered if I might take a moment of your time to ask more about Gertrude and how she became Lady Wilson?" He leaned an elbow on the counter in an effort to make their conversation seem informal.

Theodore chuckled. "You're asking about the contest?" he countered in a lower voice.

Adam seemed reluctant to agree. "That... and how she came to be chosen."

"Ah," the clerk responded, his bushy brows wagging. "Well, back then, the contestants had to share their talent."

"Talent?" Adam repeated, before he remembered the list he had found in the box.

"At the fair. The ones who could sing, sang a song. Those who could play, did so."

"How did they play?" Adam asked in surprise.

"They moved the piano-forte from Mrs. Stafford's mother's salon into the village square. She about had apoplexy, fearin' they would drop it," Theodore explained.

"And if the contestants didn't sing or… or play?" Adam prompted.

"Those who could paint or draw showed off their artwork in an exhibition," the clerk replied. "There were easels set up on the stage, you see, so Sir Winston could review the art in between the songs and such."

"I see," Adam murmured. "So they knew to bring the paintings with them?"

Theodore shrugged. "Or they created something the day of the contest. I seem to remember there were two young ladies who drew portraits of Sir Winston."

When he didn't elaborate, Adam leaned closer to his cousin. "Were they any good?" he asked, not sure he wanted anyone to be doing a drawing of him.

Theodore grimaced. "One was actually a good depiction of your grandfather. The other..." he gave his head a shake, "not so much."

"And neither one of the artists were chosen," Adam stated.

Shaking his head, Theodore said, "Gertie played the piano and sang like a bird."

"So... she was the clear winner?" Adam guessed.

His cousin guffawed as he once again shook his head. "Probably not." When he noted Adam's look of confusion, he said, "First, you need to know that my grandmother was determined she get her sister married off to Sir Winston."

Adam's brows furrowed. "Why?" he asked, suspicion evident in his voice.

"The reason wasn't nefarious, sir. But the family needed work. Jobs were hard to come by around these parts back then. Getting Gertie married off to the baronet meant my father and mother had positions in the Wilson Hall household. My brother, too. Landed a job as a stable boy."

"Hmph. So... how was it Sir Winston came to choose Gertrude?"

"She cheated. Or rather, my mother did."

Adam gave a start, his brows furrowed in confusion. "How was that even possible?"

Theodore shrugged. "Gossip, sir. Mother knew exactly how to besmirch someone without saying anything too terribly bad about them. Mostly left people questioning a young lady's suitability, if you catch my meaning."

Staring at the clerk with a look of disbelief, Adam recalled his great aunt Gaby—Gabriella—with fondness. She had been his grandmother's lady's maid, seeing to Gertie's clothes and styling her hair and wigs in outlandish coiffures for evening meals and balls in

London. "I cannot imagine her doing that," Adam murmured.

"Them young ladies would do whatever they had to back then to land a titled man," Theodore claimed. "There weren't very many bachelors available back then, given the wars and all."

"And now?" Adam prompted. "Would they stoop to such measures now, do you suppose?"

His cousin shrugged. "Not those who live around here, but those chits in Torquay? I do hope you won't be considering any of them, sir."

Adam inhaled, intending to ask what it was about young ladies in Torquay that had everyone warning him against them when Theodore slid his copy of the *Torquay Chronicle* on the counter so it rested between them.

Glancing down, Adam winced when he noticed the headline of an article near the top of the news-sheet.

Tiffs Erupt Among Lady Wilson Contestants

"Oh, good God," he murmured before he continued reading.

Local lady's shop Madame Josephine's was forced to close for a time yesterday when verbal sparring and a fight ensued between several young ladies. Madame Josephine explained they were arguing over her limited selection of gowns and hats, presumedly to wear for the Lady Wilson contest scheduled for the Cockington village fair next Monday.

Constable Jones, who was treated for injuries suffered when he attempted to rescue a Parisian dinner gown from one of those involved, said he barely escaped the shop with his life. He described the scene as chaotic and was forced to flee when two of the combatants began pummeling him with their reticules.

"They was screamin' and scratchin' each other with their fingernails," he was quoted as saying while a local physician applied a plaster to his bleeding cheek. "If he values his life, Sir Adam had best not choose any of them to be his wife."

Arrangements for restitution have already been made with two of those accused. They both claimed they were merely desperate to make a good impression on the baronet. "Who wouldn't want a titled man for a husband?" asked one of those involved in the fight. "And the chance to live in the capital?"

Madame Josephine planned to reopen her shop today but said she is refusing entrance to young *ladies until after the village fair is over. Charges against two others involved in the tiff are still pending.*

Adam looked up at his cousin and scoffed. "That's it. No contestants from Torquay," he announced as he tapped a finger on the news-sheet.

"Thought you'd agree, sir," Theodore replied. "In the meantime, have you given a thought as to whom you *will* choose?"

Adam blinked. "I don't even know who plans to enter," he admitted with a grimace. He audibly sighed. "I may have made a huge mistake announcing this contest. I had no intention of it causing this kind of reaction. This sort of trouble."

"Of course not, sir," Theodore agreed before clearing his throat. "I probably shouldn't say anything, but I thought you should know that the flyer that Mrs. McNulty posted in my window went missing the day after she was here."

Adam glanced back at the window. "Who took it?"

Theodore shrugged. "Couldn't say, sir. Probably some chit who didn't want any competition."

"Oh, well that's just..." Adam started to say when he remembered what his housekeeper had told him about the possibility of the flyers being stolen. "Mr.

Baker did print some extras in the event some went missing," he murmured. "I'll have one dropped off when someone from the household is next in town."

"Very good, sir. In the meantime, was there something I can help you find?"

About to reply in the negative—he had only come to ask his cousin about his grandmother and the contest—Adam reconsidered. "Perhaps there is. I'm not sure if you heard, but I've hired Mrs. Longburn to act as governess for my daughter."

Although he had already heard the gossip from Mrs. Stafford and Mrs. Baker and then from his wife, Theodore pretended it was news. "Oh, good choice, sir. Mrs. Longburn is an impeccable woman. Educated, too. Why, she was just in here buying embroidery thread and a hoop yesterday. I think she plans to teach Miss Penelope how to sew."

Adam straightened at hearing this bit of news. "Hmph," he replied. "Well, the servants at Wilson Hall have cleared out the top floor to create a sort of playroom for my daughter. Although there are some furnishings up there, it's rather sparse. There's very little in the way of decoration or... accessories."

The clerk seemed to consider the comment a moment before he asked, "Does your daughter have a sewing basket?"

Adam shook his head. "I don't think so. Alice had one, but..." He sighed as he rolled his eyes. "Her dog tore it to pieces."

"A sewing basket, then," Theodore said as he winced at hearing what had happened. "Mrs. Longburn only bought a couple of skeins of thread. Maybe more colors? Some needles? A good candle lamp for extra light."

Shrugging, Adam said, "Sounds good. Can you put it all together whilst I look around?"

"Of course, sir." Theodore stepped from behind the counter and went about collecting the items while Adam made his way around the store. By the time he had returned, he had a collection of oddities to add to the sewing basket and embroidery threads Theodore had pulled from the shelves.

The clerk wrote out a receipt and announced the total, which had Adam digging into his purse. "I prefer to pay now, if that's all right."

"Of course, sir. May I ask when it is you plan to give the basket to Miss Penelope?" Theodore queried, anxious for any gossip. "Is it for a special occasion perhaps?"

Adam paused as he pulled a five-pound note from his purse. "I had thought to give it to her when I return to Wilson Hall, but now that you mention it, her birthday is tomorrow. Perhaps I'll wait until then."

"Very good, sir," Theodore replied. He watched as the baronet took his leave, wondering at the other items Sir Adam had purchased besides the sewing notions, basket, and candle lamp.

The pad of drawing paper, two charcoal pencils, a slate, and sticks of colored chalk made perfect sense since Mrs. Longburn was now employed as a teacher for her charge. But he couldn't sort the reason for the pair of candlesticks, a ceramic vase, and silk flowers.

What did the baronet have planned?

CHAPTER 16
A RUSE REVEALED

few minutes later

"Well, did he see it?" William Coulsden asked before he had even shut the door to the mercantile behind him.

Theodore looked up from his copy of the *Torquay Chronicle* and gave a start at seeing his breathless brother. "He did, but what are *you* doing in here?" he asked, his gaze darting to the window to see that the Wilson coach was still parked out front.

"Baronet's gone into the butcher's shop, so I have a minute or two," William replied. "Smithton is watchin' the 'orses."

"Well, I hope you gave a copy of the fake *Chronicle* to Mr. Fraser."

William nodded. "Switched 'em out 'afore Jimmy

could deliver them to anyone in the village," he replied. "Burned the real ones when I got back to Wilson Hall."

The clerk grinned and then shook his head. "I think it's going to work. He read the whole article about the fight at Madame Josephine's while he was standing here," Theodore claimed in a hoarse whisper.

"I still can't believe you convinced Mr. Baker to print those fake copies of the *Chronicle*," his brother said with a chuckle.

Rubbing his thumb and forefinger together, Theodore said, "Money talks. Anything to ensure a local lady wins the contest."

"A *certain* local lady, remember," William whispered.

"I wish you could have been there at the print shop last night," Theodore said with a grin. "It was rather funny writing up the false article with Baker. His wife was there—she was suspicious about him going back to the shop after dinner—so he allowed her to come along to prove he wasn't diddlin' anyone," he explained as he rolled his eyes. "Thought for sure the gig was up, but she was laughing so hard while she was helping us come up with the words, I thought she was going to have a coronary."

William's eyes rounded with worry. "Mrs. Baker

knows?" he asked in dismay. "But... Mildred Baker is a gossip. She'll tell everyone—"

"When I asked Baker if we had reason to worry that she might spill the beans, he assured me she would have done something similar if we didn't," Theodore claimed. "Apparently, she's all for Mrs. Longburn becoming the next Lady Wilson." He glanced up again, wanting to be sure the baronet and Mr. Smithton weren't waiting outside for his brother to return to the coach. "Why did he come into town today?" he asked, referring to Sir Adam.

"We was just at the boarding house," William replied. "He had an appointment with the parson. I overheard Reverend Trayfor talkin' about Mrs. Long-burn," he explained. "Miss Barrows let me sit outside the parlor to wait for the baronet, and I heard most of what was discussed." His eyes suddenly rounded. "Did you know she is married to the parson?"

Theodore blinked. "Mrs. Longburn?" he asked in shock.

William scoffed. "No. Miss Barrows. She's really Mrs. Trayfor. Turns out, they've been husband and wife for *years*."

Theodore's eyes widened as he guffawed. "The parson is pretending to have an *affaire* when he's really married," he said with a grin. "Gotta appreciate a man of the cloth with a sense of humor," he added as he chuckled.

Glancing back at the window, William suddenly straightened. "I have to go. Sir Adam is coming across the road right now."

"Whatever you do, make sure there's a fake copy of the *Chronicle* at Wilson Hall. Don't want him finding a real one," Theodore whispered.

"It's already in his study," William assured him. "Saw Harris take it in," he added before he hurried out to the coach. He opened the door for the baronet. "Sorry for making you wait, sir. Thought I'd give my regards to my brother whilst I was here."

Adam nodded. "Not a problem, Mr. Coulsden," he replied before he glanced over in the direction of the butcher's shop. "Might you have any idea who has taken the Lady Wilson contest flyers out of the windows here in town?"

"Sir?" William asked, pretending surprise.

"Mr. Fraser was unaware the flyer was even missing from his window," Adam remarked. "The one that was in the mercantile is gone as well."

William pretended ignorance. "Why, I watched Mrs. McNulty put those notices in the windows myself," he replied. "Prob'ly removed by some chit from Torquay," he added in disgust. "Or Livermead." He waited until

Adam had climbed into the coach before he said, "If you have any extras flyers, I can bring them to town. Post them for you."

The baronet seemed to think on the suggestion for a moment. "I don't think that will be necessary, but thank you for offering."

"Very good, sir." William closed the coach door. He joined Mr. Smithton on the driver's seat, wondering what his master had in mind.

CHAPTER 17
BOXES ARE OPENED

*B*ack at Wilson Hall

Lost in thought, Adam was jerked back to the here and now when the coach stuttered to a halt outside of Wilson Hall. Although he appreciated the time he had spent speaking with Michael Trayfor, he was now left feeling doubt about his decision to remarry, or at least the manner in which he had decided to find a wife.

The idea to hold a contest had been a lark. It had worked for his grandfather, although now that he knew the truth of how Gertrude Amherst had come to be his grandmother, he had begun to wonder if he shouldn't cancel the contest and go about finding a wife in the more traditional manner.

He could go to London for the Season. Attend balls

and *soirées*. Dance with young ladies and court one of them.

Not having courted Alice—he and she had always simply known they would marry one another—he didn't relish the idea. In fact, if he didn't require an heir, he would simply live out the remainder of his days at Wilson Hall, doing business by post and courier or through a secretary and raising Penelope until it was time for her come-out.

He was in the middle of groaning loudly at the thought of her old enough to marry when William opened the coach door. "Are you all right, sir?" the groom asked in alarm.

"Have you ever been married, Mr. Coulsden?" Adam asked as he handed over the crate of items he had purchased at the mercantile. He pulled the sewing basket from the wooden box and tucked it under one arm.

"No, sir. Can't say as I have," Williams replied, hefting the crate onto one shoulder.

Adam stepped down from the coach. "Ever been tempted to marry?"

William looked as if he couldn't decide how to answer. "Truth be told, sir, I have had my eye on a particular woman for some time, but..." He sighed and gave his master a shrug.

"Really?" Adam asked in surprise. "Anyone I know?"

William's face took on a reddish cast. "Mrs. McNulty, sir. I'd appreciate if you didn't say anythin' to anyone seein' as how, well,... I haven't got the nerve to ask just yet."

"Hmph," Adam replied as he straightened. "You're not getting any younger, and neither is she, Coulsden," he warned. "Seems if you want her for a wife, you'd best make your intentions known."

The groom seemed surprised at hearing the baronet's pronouncement. "Yes, sir," William replied. "I suppose you're gettin' anxious for the Lady Wilson contest?"

Anxious wasn't quite the word Adam would have used at that point. "I suppose," he said without enthusiasm. "This contest has certainly stirred up trouble, though."

"Oh, would you be referring to that incident in Torquay, sir?" At seeing Sir Adam's brow lift, the groom smirked. "My brother told me about it, whilst I was waitin' for you," William explained. "Can't say I'm surprised. Them chits in Torquay and Livermead, well, they're not like the nice young ladies we have here in Cockington, if you catch my meaning."

Adam furrowed a brow. "You're the third person to

make such a claim on this day," he accused. "Makes me think the locals are determined to see me wed to a Cockington lass."

William blinked. "Well, that would be preferable, sir. Otherwise, you'll end up livin' over in London."

Giving a start, Adam stared at the groom. "And why do you say that?"

Waving a hand in the direction of Torquay, William said, "Them chits from the larger towns only want to marry you so they can move ta the capital, sir."

It was Adam's turn to blink. "But, I have no plans to move back to London," he stated.

William shrugged. "They don't know that, sir."

"Hmph." Without another word, Adam made his way into Wilson Hall.

"Sir? Where would you like me to take this here crate?" William called out.

About to head into his study, Adam turned to see the groom still standing on the top step outside the front door. "Fourth floor. Give it to Mrs. Longburn." He paused a moment. "No, wait. Give it to my daughter," he said with a gleam in his eye.

"Yes, sir."

Adam watched Harris close the front door and then realized the groom would take the box around to the back of the house to use the servants' entrance.

Settling into the chair behind his desk, Adam lifted the copy of the *Torquay Chronicle* that Harris had delivered earlier that morning. About to lean back to read the rest of the issue, he decided instead to make his way to the fourth floor.

He wanted to see Penelope's response when William delivered the crate.

"Hello?" William called out when he emerged from the servants' stairs into the Wilson Hall ballroom, the wooden crate still perched on his shoulder. "I have a delivery for a Miss Penelope Wilson."

Charlotte and Penelope looked up in unison from the book they had been reading. "Mr. Coulsden," Charlotte said as she stood. Penelope hurried over to the groom, bouncing excitedly.

"A delivery for *me*?" she asked with a toothless grin.

"Indeed. I had orders to deliver it to you and only you, Miss Penelope. Where would you like it?"

"What have you there?" Charlotte asked as she joined the young girl, her gaze indicating surprise.

"Can't say as I know," the groom replied with a grin.

"Well then, perhaps on the floor of our make-believe parlor," Charlotte suggested.

She watched as William lowered the box onto the Turkish carpet and Penelope bent over to study the contents. The groom stepped back, but his curiosity had him remaining nearby.

"Oh, Charlotte," Penelope said with excitement. "There's all sorts of things in here."

"Well then, I suppose you should start with what's on top," Charlotte said, her own curiosity piqued.

Penelope lifted a slate from the box. "What is it?" she asked as she held it up.

Charlotte inhaled softly. "It's a slate, darling. Oh, with a bit of chalk, this will make doing your letters so much easier," she said as she took the slate from her charge. "You can erase what you've written with a rag and use it again and again," she explained. "I don't suppose there's any chalk in there?"

Already diving in for the next items, Penelope was giggling as she pulled out several sticks of colored chalk. "There is. I can do my lessons now," she squealed as she spun around. She handed the chalk to Charlotte who took it over to the classroom area and placed the items on the small table around which she had been teaching Penelope. She hadn't even returned to the parlor area when she saw Penelope holding up a ceramic vase.

"Well, that's certainly unexpected," Charlotte remarked. "But it will be perfect on the fireplace mantel, don't you think?"

"Oh, yes," Penelope replied happily, already pulling the next item out of the box. "Here are the flowers to go into it." She was very nearly bouncing as she held out the bouquet of silk flowers.

"These are beautiful," Charlotte murmured as she moved to one of the side tables. She was arranging the bouquet of multicolored silk blooms when Penelope squealed again.

"Really, Penelope, you're being quite loud," she admonished. But she nearly joined the girl in squealing when she saw the drawing pad that Penelope held.

"There are charcoal pencils, too," the tyke said as she spun around in delight.

"Goodness, we'll have you learning how to draw in no time," Charlotte said as she placed the vase of flowers on the fireplace mantel. She dared a glance at William, who seemed to be having as much fun as Penelope as she revealed the items in the box.

"Surely there can't be anything else in that—"

"Candlesticks, Charlotte," Penelope said as she held up the pair of ornate silver candlesticks. "They'll be perfect on the mantel with the flowers," she added as she did the honors and, standing on tip toe, placed them on either side of the vase.

But Charlotte's attention had gone to the other side of the room. She had sensed someone watching them, and before he'd had a chance to better hide himself, she spotted Sir Adam peeking around the door frame.

"Whom do we have to thank for this generous largesse?" Charlotte asked of the groom, whose smile was as wide as Penelope's.

"Sir Adam, ma'am," he said in a low voice. "He just came from the village not a quarter hour ago." He bent and picked up the empty crate. "I'll be gettin' this box out of your way now," he said before he bowed and headed towards the servants' stairs.

"Thank you, Mr. Coulsden," Penelope called out before she giggled and hurried over to Charlotte. "Isn't it all just perfect now?" she asked as she held up a candle lamp.

"Yes. Yes, it is," Charlotte agreed. Her gaze darted to the other side of the ballroom, but if Sir Adam was still there, he was completely hidden from view. "You'll have to thank your father when you see him at dinner this evening," she murmured.

"I can't decide if I want to learn how to draw or do

my writing lesson," Penelope said as they made their way back to the classroom area.

"Good, because we're going to finish your reading lesson first," Charlotte replied with a grin. She took the candle lamp from her charge.

Penelope's expression drooped, but she dutifully sat in her chair at the table and resumed reading her primer out loud.

Leaning against the wall at the top of the stairs, Adam took a moment to relish the moments his daughter had discovered each and every item in the wooden crate. Had he any idea of how she would react, he would have seen to the purchases months ago.

The sound of her joy was infectious. It had him grinning. He could barely hold back a chuckle as he remembered how she had bounced about and spun around over finding something as simple as a slate among the treasures from the mercantile.

Remembering he had a box of his own yet to open, Adam quietly made his way down the main stairs and back to his study.

He lifted the box marked "Alice" onto his desk and took a deep breath before he removed the lid. He inhaled the scent he associated with his late wife, nearly cursing aloud at how his throat threatened to close.

Perhaps this wasn't such a good idea.

He hadn't cried over Alice's death in several years, but at that moment, he struggled with his emotions. Before tears could blur his sight, he stared down at a collection of familiar items and some others he was sure he hadn't seen before.

He pulled out her white, gilt-edged jewel box, studying it as if he were surprised at finding it in the carton rather than on a dresser in the mistress suite upstairs.

London, he remembered then. These were items that had been in her suite at their Mayfair townhouse.

A comb and brush set and the salver on which they had sat on her dressing table were followed by a wooden box of cosmetics. He scoffed, never having remembered Alice wearing lip color or kohl on her lashes. Given the number of pots in the wooden box, he realized she had used them. Frequently. Some of the pots were nearly empty.

He moved aside a stack of embroidered hankies to pull out the simple diamond tiara he had purchased for her upon their wedding. He studied the headpiece a moment before setting it aside, remembering how Alice had reacted with such joy when he had placed it upon her head before their first ball as a married couple.

Next, he pulled out a slim hinged box, and he swallowed. Knowing what was inside—he had purchased the sapphire parure for Alice upon learning she was expecting his child—Adam set it aside and regarded the last remaining item in the box.

The fabric-covered book was worn, the edges of its front cover threadbare. A simple wooden peg and fabric loop kept it closed.

Adam took a seat at his desk and undid the book's fastening. The book fell open as if the pages had been ready to burst out. Long paragraphs topped with dates at the the upper edge of each page were written in Alice's even, perfect script.

Her diary, he realized as his gaze went to a series of entries near the back of the book. There were several pages of her writing beyond the one that lay open before him, and behind that, the remaining sheets were blank. He only stayed on the pages that had opened before him because he saw his name at the top.

Adam will make an excellent father. I must admit that I did not believe he would care one way or the other if I ever gave him a child, but I now realize he is over the moon happy with my condition.

If only I could survive to see my babe grow up.

Adam leaned forward as he lifted his gaze from the page, stunned at what he had just read. "Damnation," he muttered before he resumed reading.

Three physicians are in agreement as is Lottie. I think I feel more sorry for her than I do for myself. She could always see the frailty which others have attributed to my petite size. She begged me not to wed. Begged me not to find myself in such a condition. But how could I prevent such a circumstance? I certainly didn't wish to. My Adam is an attentive husband, and his title requires an heir.

Carrying this babe has been a blessing. I pray it be a boy, and although some will claim I have made some sort of sacrifice to bring him into this world, I have not. Truly. I only wish the best for him and for his father.

As for Lottie, I will miss her counsel where I am to go. I will miss her gentle ribbing—her teases are entertaining rather than cutting. I will miss her strong shoulders which I have dampened far too many times with my tears.

She must be strong always, for I have made her

promise she will see to it this babe is raised properly.

If only she and Adam were not so cold to one another. How can the two people I love most in this world be so at odds?

Oh, I remember now. It is because I chose a husband over a best friend with whom to spend these past two years. Instead of directing her disappointment toward me, she aimed it at him. So like poor Lottie to blame him over me when I am the one clearly at fault. But then, she is my very best friend.

Continuing to read until there were no more entries in the diary, Adam sat back in his chair and wept. *She knew she would die*, he thought, as sadness warred with anger, as annoyance replaced the anger, and finally exhaustion settled over him like a cold blanket.

When Harris announced dinner, he simply stared at the servant and shook his head. "Not tonight, Harris."

The butler furrowed his bushy brows before he gave a bow and said, "Very good, sir."

CHAPTER 18
DINNER INTERRUPTED

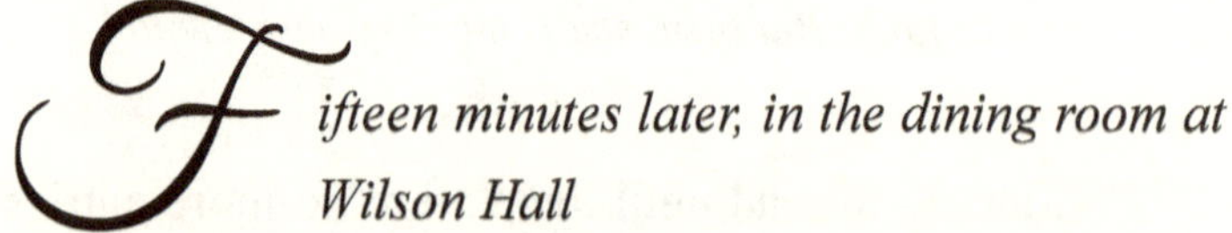

ifteen minutes later, in the dining room at Wilson Hall

Penelope was very nearly in tears when her father didn't appear for dinner that evening. "But I have to thank him for all the gifts he sent," she said when Harris appeared and announced that the master of the house wouldn't be joining them.

"Is something wrong?" Charlotte asked, nearly halfway out of her chair.

Harris seemed torn as to how to reply. "He opened his late wife's box from London this afternoon."

Charlotte inhaled softly. "Oh, dear." Although she knew of the box from having seen it in the ballroom the week before, she had no idea of its contents. Her first thought was that it was filled with Alice's gowns.

She should have known there would be other items in Alice's bedchamber in the Wilson townhouse in London. Remembering the layout of the room from having been a frequent visitor, she recalled Alice's jewel box sitting on the dressing table. Her cosmetics box. The parure Sir Adam had bestowed on her when she announced she was going to have a baby. Her diary on her bedside table.

Gasping, Charlotte stared at the butler. "Oh, no," she whispered.

"What's wrong, Charlotte?" Penelope asked from where she sat at the middle of the table.

Almost saying she was about to be sacked, Charlotte straightened and forced a smile she didn't feel. "It nothing, Miss Penelope. Eat your dinner," she encouraged.

Although she had been hungry when they entered the dining room, she in her very best teal dinner gown and Penelope dressed in a white frock with a white smock and matching stockings, Charlotte now felt as if she had dressed for her dismissal.

She drained her wine in a few gulps and forced down a few bites of the fish course before she glanced over at Penelope to discover tears streaming down the girl's face.

"Oh, Penelope," she murmured as she pulled a

hanky from her pocket. "Don't cry. There's nothing to cry about," she whispered.

"Then why are *you* crying?" Penelope asked as she wiped her cheeks with the hanky.

Charlotte gave a start. "I... oh, dear. I didn't know I was," she replied, a watery grin appearing too late.

"I want to see my father," Penelope said. Before Charlotte could reply, the girl was off her chair and heading for the door. Charlotte followed, but she had to pause as the dining room seemed to spin before she could get her feet firmly beneath her.

Had she drunk too much wine?

Once she had straightened and the room no longer threatened to upend her, she calmly made her way out of the dining room and down the corridor. She had caught a glimpse of white disappearing into the study, and she slowly made her way in that direction.

"Father?" she heard before she reached the study. She could only imagine what the poor girl would find.

Adam, passed out on his desk from having drunk too much brandy.

Adam, passed out on the floor in front of the fire-place, having impaled himself on the poker.

Adam, passed out in a chair from having cried himself to sleep.

Instead, she found Penelope sitting on her father's

lap, her head on his shoulder and her arms wrapped around his neck. A quick glance at his desk, and she spotted Alice's jewel box and her diary. Although it was closed, she could see that its fastening had been undone.

"Thank you for the gifts you sent today," Penelope said before she kissed him on the cheek. "They make the parlor ever so special. And thank you, too, for the school things. Charlotte said she will teach me how to draw, and today I used the slate to learn more letters," she claimed. "X, Y and Z."

"I knew you could put them to good use," Adam said before he kissed her on the forehead. "They certainly weren't getting any use at the mercantile where I found them today."

After she kissed him on the cheek again, Penelope snuggled in his hold. "Why didn't you come to dinner, Father?" she asked.

Charlotte watched as Adam seemed to struggle with how to respond. "I learned some very sad news today," he said, his gaze darting to his desk. "I didn't wish to attend dinner until I was feeling better, and, well, now that I am, I think I will join you," he said as he leaned forward to stand. Given the weight of his daughter in his arms, he found he couldn't gain his feet, and he chuckled. "Oh, Poppet. You have grown too large for me to lift you as I once did," he said with a sigh.

It was then he noticed Charlotte standing on the study's threshold. "You look as if you've lost your best friend," he commented before he winced and then sighed. "Apologies. That was—"

"Exactly how I felt," Charlotte replied quickly. "When I learned you weren't going to join us for dinner. Miss Penelope has been looking forward to having dinner with you all day," she explained, wishing she no longer wanted to spend time in his company. It would make her parting so much easier. As it was, leaving Penelope would be heartbreaking enough. "She was most appreciative of your gifts."

Adam regarded her a moment before he dipped his head. "I saw," he admitted. "But then, I think you knew that." Having lowered Penelope to the floor so he could stand, he now lifted his daughter back into his arms and kissed her on the cheek.

A blush colored Charlotte's face. "I'm not sure, but I think your groom was almost as excited as Miss Penelope. I've never seen a grown man so curious and happy at what came out of a wooden crate," she commented.

"He'll be even happier if we can get him wed to

Mrs. McNulty," Adam remarked, his brows furrowing when he noticed tears on Charlotte's cheeks.

Charlotte gave a start. "You know about that, sir?"

Adam chuckled, glad for a reason to shed his hours of melancholy. "I forced it out of him today. Poor sod."

"Father, what's a sod?"

Adam winced. "An unfortunate man," he replied, his attention on Charlotte as he made the comment.

Uncomfortable at the way Adam stared at her, Charlotte did her best to suppress a sob and dropped her gaze to the floor. "If you're planning to dismiss me, sir, could you just get it over with so I can make arrangements?" she asked in a hoarse whisper.

Jerking head back as if he'd been slapped, Adam shook his head. "I've no intention of dismissing you," he replied, wondering from where she'd gotten the idea she was to be let go. "Besides, it would make it terribly difficult for you to do what you promised Alice you would do."

Charlotte's eyes rounded before her gaze darted to the diary. "You know about that?"

He nodded. "I read her diary." He gave his head a shake. "Not all of it, of course. The last entries, mostly." Pausing a moment, he added, "A bit of a shock, I'll admit."

Her face nearly as red as her hair, Charlotte wiped away a tear from one cheek. "You don't hate me, sir?"

Clearing his throat, Adam shook his head. "I could not hate someone who held Alice in such high regard. I'm only sorry she could never share with me what she did with you," he said, miffed that Alice had kept her frailty from him. That she hadn't allowed her physicians to inform him she wouldn't survive childbirth. "As for her assessment that I was cold towards you, I must take exception. If I ever seemed so, please believe me when I say that I never knowingly gave you a cut, direct or otherwise."

Charlotte's eyes once again widened as she swallowed. "I never thought you did, sir," she murmured.

Adam regarded her with a furrowed brow before he nodded. "Good. Then let's go eat. I'm starving," he said.

"The fish course was served a few minutes ago," Charlotte said. She was about to turn around, but she dared another glance at his desk, wondering about the diary.

What had Alice written about her?

CHAPTER 19
A DIARY REVEALS TOO MUCH

*D*uring dinner

Announcing he wished to join the ladies in the parlor for their tea after dinner, Sir Adam was gladdened when his daughter beamed in delight and said he was welcome to join them.

He wondered at Charlotte's tepid response. He had hoped their brief conversation in the study might have cleared up any misunderstanding she had with him, but she had spent the meal allowing Penelope to practice her dinner conversation as she seemed lost in thought.

"Can we have our after dinner tea in my parlor on the fourth floor?" Penelope asked during the dessert course.

Adam exchanged a quick glance with Charlotte.

"You think it would be warm enough up there?" he countered.

"We could light a fire in the fireplace," Penelope suggested. "I wish for you to see how it all looks with the decorations you bought for me."

When Charlotte didn't put voice to a protest, Adam cleared his throat. "How about I join you for your morning tea up there?" he suggested. "That way, it will be light enough for me to see everything. Right now, that entire floor is very dark."

"Oh, that's a good point, sir," Charlotte remarked, the first words she had spoken since before the main course. "Besides, I think we left things a bit of a mess this afternoon after our last lesson," she added with a wince.

"Oh?" Adam replied, his curiosity piqued.

"I spread out all my drawings on the floor," Penelope admitted, her shoulders lifting as her head dipped between them.

"I should like to see them," Adam said. "And when I come for tea, I should like to bring your birthday gifts."

Penelope's eyes widened as she nearly squealed. "Gifts?" she repeated. "More gifts?"

For the first time since they'd sat down to dinner, Charlotte displayed a happy expression. "Six years," she said. "So hard to believe it's been that long."

Adam stared at her a moment before he nodded. "Yes, it is hard to believe," he murmured.

*L*ater that night Charlotte listened for the last of the servants' doors at the opposite end of the hall to close and for the household to grow quiet before she slipped out of her apartment. Holding a candle lamp before her, she crept down the stairs and made her way to the study, her night rail and dressing gown billowing behind her as she quickened her steps.

Finding the door open, she paused before peering in, wondering if Adam might have come back to the study after their evening in the parlor.

He'd been so surprised when Penelope sat at the piano forté and played the short lullaby Charlotte had taught her earlier that day, and yet his attention hadn't been on his daughter. It had been on Charlotte. As if he knew something she did not.

Determined to learn what Alice had written about her during her last days, Charlotte made her way to his desk and found the diary where he had left it. The clasp was still undone.

As she settled into his leather chair, the scents of amber and spice surrounding her, Charlotte nearly gasped when she lifted the book and it opened of its own accord.

Breathless, she began to read the same entries Adam had read earlier that day. Her hands shook as they turned the pages. Tears blinded her eyes. Blinking them away, she nearly choked when she read one of the last entries.

I have finally determined why it is my dear Lottie holds my Adam in such contempt. For it is not contempt at all, but a clever manner in which to hide her regard for him. I believe she loves him. Secretly, of course, because she cannot share with me that she holds him in such high regard.

But how could she not love him? I have espoused his good manners and characteristics the entire time I have known him, perhaps because I felt the need to make her understand just how it is he could capture my heart, body, and soul. Why it is he could be the only husband for me.

Perhaps after I am gone from this earth, she will let down her guard and free her heart. If she does as she has promised, she will not only be seeing to it this babe is educated, but she will see to it that

Adam is not left alone in this world. He would not do well alone, but then, neither would she. It would be best if they find one another. If not, Cupid had best pick up his bow, draw an arrow, and do his job. I will always be grateful for the arrows he shot at Adam and me.

Charlotte set the diary down and pushed it away as she struggled to breathe. She had never admitted her desire for Adam to Alice. To anyone. She had never put voice one way or the other to her thoughts on the man. Never admitted she had fallen in love. And yet Alice had seen right through her carefully crafted ambivalence.

Damn her.

For Charlotte was fairly sure Adam now knew her secret. He had read the diary that afternoon. He hadn't dismissed her, though. Other than the comment about his belief that he had never been cold towards her, Adam hadn't mentioned anything else of what he had learned from the diary.

Perhaps he thought it all a fiction.

Or perhaps he knew better than to bring up a matter of the heart with an employee.

After a few minutes, when her breathing had returned to normal, Charlotte's gaze went to the Lady

Wilson contest flyers on the corner of the desk. Surprised to see them there—she had thought Mrs. McNulty had posted all of them—Charlotte feared they were the ones she had collected from the various shops. None showed signs of folding, though, and she relaxed once again. These were simply extra copies.

That these flyers weren't posted meant they weren't being seen by anyone in the village or neighboring towns. The edict that no women from Torquay would be considered at the contest meant fewer women would be entering. There would be less competition.

Knowing now that she had Alice's blessing, Charlotte made a decision.

If she had any hope of becoming Lady Wilson, she had to enter the contest. And depending on Sir Adam's thoughts on the matter, she might have to be the only one to enter.

She could ask him, of course. He was close by. But she thought it best they both sleep on the matter.

*M*eanwhile
From where he sat in the corner of his study, gowned in his dark banyan, Adam was sure his presence would be discovered at any moment by his daughter's governess.

He knew Charlotte had spotted the diary on his desk earlier that evening. Knew from her strange behavior during their dinner that evening that Charlotte Longburn's curiosity would get the best of her. He was fairly sure that same curiosity would have her coming to the study to read the diary.

Even if she didn't appear, it was still his intention to drink a glass of brandy as he considered what to do now that he knew more about the confounding woman. More about Alice's regard for her best friend. More about why it was Charlotte had come to Cockington when she had.

Well, Charlotte had succumbed to her curiosity. She hadn't even skulked when entering the study. Wearing nothing more than a night rail and a thin dressing gown, she had simply sailed in and taken a seat in his leather chair. What was worse was the fact that her red hair was loose, the long strands extending well past her shoulders. In the circle of light from her candle lamp, it practically glowed with the colors of fire.

Deciding he wouldn't announce his presence, Adam did struggle with sitting still as his cock responded. That was his penance for sitting not twelve feet away whilst spying on Charlotte.

For a moment, he imagined lifting her onto his desk after sweeping it clear of everything on the top of it. Of kissing her mouth and breasts with abandon. Of nibbling her nipples through the thin fabric of the night rail. He was fairly sure the muslim would provide the perfect texture through which to worry them into tight buds with his tongue. Not like silk, which would prove too smooth to provide the sort of pleasure he wished to cause.

Once the space at the top of her thighs was throbbing with need—he'd be sure of it with the stroke of a finger—he'd shove his cock into her and ride her to a quick and pleasurable release.

That would be her punishment for encroaching on his quiet time.

Who was he kidding, though? He wanted her here. He wanted her to learn the truth. Wanted her to know what Alice believed, even if it was a fiction.

She was reading the diary now. Reading it and weeping, sniffling and whispering. *She sounds just like I did when I read it*, he thought as he nearly groaned in discomfort.

When she closed the book and pushed it away, as if it had burned her, Adam was about to announce his presence. He stopped, though, when she turned her attention on the contest flyers on his desk.

Curiosity had him freezing in place. Whatever could she be thinking as she stared at them?

When she finally rose from the desk and lifted the candle lamp, Adam watched as she made her way to the door. About to sigh in relief, he couldn't when she turned and said, "Good night, Sir Adam," before she took her leave.

He rolled his eyes, realizing she had probably known he was there all along. "Good night, Mrs. Longburn."

When the sounds of her retreating footsteps faded, Adam leaned back in the chair, slid his hand beneath his banyan, and took his member in hand. It took only moments for the ecstasy to overwhelm his senses as he imagined Charlotte's hand gripping him. As he imagined driving his engorged cock into her until she felt the same overwhelming pleasure he experienced. Until his name sounded on her lips and they wrapped their arms around one another.

When slumber took him, the dream continued. When he awoke in the middle of the night, he felt bereft at discovering he was alone in the chair.

Cursing softly, he made his way up to his bedchamber. Determined he not have to live through another night like this, he promised himself that in less than a week, he would be sharing the bed with someone else.

In the meantime, he would have to be satisfied by holding onto a pillow.

CHAPTER 20
A SEWING BASKET FOR A
BIRTHDAY

The following morning, tea time

Just as Charlotte expected, Penelope had a hard time concentrating as her governess tried to teach her how to write words with four letters.

"It's my birthday," Penelope reminded her.

"Yes, I know, darling. You're six years old now, and it looks as if your bottom teeth are coming in," Charlotte remarked as she held Penelope's chin with her thumb and forefinger. "Why, in a few weeks, you won't even know your front teeth were missing."

"Another one is loose," Penelope said as she pushed on an incisor.

"Oh, you'll have to let your father know," Charlotte replied, wincing at seeing Penelope's tongue push against the loose tooth.

"Know what?" Adam asked as he joined them from the main stairs at the opposite end of the room. He carried a box wrapped box in fabric on one arm. At the same moment, Harris appeared at the top of the servants' stairs carrying a tea tray.

"Father! Another tooth is loose," Penelope lisped as she hurried to join him. She gasped. "Is that for me?" She bounced excitedly, her loose tooth forgotten.

Adam regarded the box as if he had just noticed it resting on his arm. "Why I do believe it is. Happy birthday, Poppet," he said as he gave it to her. He turned his attention to Charlotte, pleased to see color come to her cheeks when he said, "Good morning, Mrs. Longburn."

"Good morning, sir," she replied with a self-conscious grin. "So good of you to join us for tea this morning."

"I appreciate the invitation," he countered, as he moved toward the settee. He paused to study the small drawings that covered part of the floor, a chuckle sounding when he recognized himself in one of them.

"A man bearing gifts is always welcome for tea," Charlotte replied. She took a seat and moved to pour the tea, her gaze going to Penelope.

"I'll have to remember that," Adam said as he turned a huge smile on his daughter and then took a seat next to Charlotte.

She offered Adam a cup and then watched as the girl unwrapped the rectangular box and then inhaled softly when the rattan sewing basket came into view.

"Be sure to open it," Adam said.

Penelope's eyes widened in delight as she turned the fastening. When she had the lid open, her mouth rounded. "Oh, Charlotte. We have every color to sew with now," she exclaimed as she pulled handfuls of embroidery thread from the box.

"Careful, Poppet, there are needles in there," her father warned.

"Needles? As in, more than one?" Charlotte asked in awe.

Adam furrowed a brow. "Three, I think. They came that way," he said as Penelope pulled out a thick paper with the needles threaded through it.

"There are tiny scissors, too, and linen, and a wooden hoop," Penelope announced, pulling out each item and to hold it up.

Charlotte dared a glance at Adam, swallowing when she saw how he gazed at his daughter. He was having nearly as much fun as Penelope as the basket revealed its treasures. "It seems I'll be adding embroidery lessons sooner than I thought," she said.

Adam gave her a quick glance. "My cousin, Mr. Coulsden—the one at the mercantile—mentioned you had purchased some thread a few days ago," Adam said. "I thought you were already teaching her."

"Well, she knows how to thread a needle and do straight stitches," Charlotte acknowledged. "But that's all, so far."

"Hmph," he murmured when Penelope stood and then joined them.

"Thank you, Father," she said as she curtsied.

"You're welcome, Poppet," he replied, reaching out to take her hand to his lips.

"Would you like a biscuit?" she asked. "Cook made my favorite for my birthday," she added as she held out the plate of lemon biscuits. Meanwhile, Charlotte poured the girl a cup of tea.

Adam helped himself to one and regarded it a moment before he said, "I've sent a note to the *Torquay Chronicle* with word that no young ladies from there or from Livermead will be welcome to enter the Lady Wilson contest."

Charlotte stared at him a moment, gasping softly. "Because of what happened at Madame Josephine's?"

He nodded. "Have you been there?"

"I have," she acknowledged. "Only a few times. Before I was married," Charlotte replied. "It's just a dress shop." She watched as Penelope stirred a lump of sugar into her tea, her pinky carefully held out.

Adam bristled at the reminder Charlotte had been married. "Do you ever recall any similar incidents? Of fights or disagreements among the ladies present?"

"Of course not," Charlotte replied. "I read the article. I cannot even imagine such an occurrence in Torquay, though. On New Bond Street in London, perhaps, at the start of a Season. But surely not in Torquay."

Adam regarded her with furrowed brows. "Are you suggesting… it didn't happen?"

Charlotte shrugged. "Given those who were quoted in the article, it obviously did. It just seems so unlikely."

"Hmph."

"Are you thinking it did not?" she asked, heartened to see how Penelope placed her tea on a side table before she climbed on the settee to sit next to her father.

"I'm not sure what to think, especially after learning the contest flyers have gone missing from the windows in Cockington," he remarked, curious as to how she would respond.

Glad she wasn't taking a sip of tea at that moment, Charlotte regarded him a moment before saying, "Well, that's rather odd."

"I thought so, too, until I realized removing the

flyers meant fewer people would know about the contest," he said.

"You think a potential contestant has pulled them from the windows?" she asked in mock alarm.

"Or someone who must really want a particular woman to become Lady Wilson," he reasoned.

It was Charlotte's turn to say, "Hmph."

"How many ladies do you think will be in the contest, Father?" Penelope asked.

Adam inhaled and considered the query a moment. "Well, if only young ladies from Cockington can enter the contest, then there won't be but a few, I suppose, which means the contest won't take very long. You'll have a chance to visit the lambs before the best one is chosen."

Penelope beamed in delight before she helped herself to another biscuit.

Adam drained his tea. "Well, I must be off. I've a shipment of silk to arrange for the shop in London," he said as he set his teacup on the low table.

"Thank you for joining us for tea," Penelope said as she hopped off the settee and curtsied.

Bending down, Adam kissed her on the cheek. "Happy birthday, Poppet. With any luck, you'll have a baby brother or sister for your birthday next year."

Penelope's eyes rounded before they turned on Charlotte. "But… what if I don't want a baby?"

Charlotte tittered as she stood. "You needn't worry about having a baby for a very long time," she said.

"She had better not," Adam said in hoarse whisper. "She's growing up far too fast as it is."

"Indeed," Charlotte agreed as she gave him a wan grin. "Good day, sir."

He aimed a curious glance in her direction before he made his way across the ballroom and to the main stairs.

Charlotte waited until he disappeared before she turned her attention to Penelope. "It's time we put one of your new gifts to use, young lady," she announced as she held up the drawing pad and pencils.

Grinning in delight, Penelope hurried to the table.

As the girl spent the afternoon drawing her doll and the tea set, Charlotte daydreamed.

CHAPTER 21
THE VILLAGE FAIR ATTRACTS
A CROWD

The day after Easter, April 20, 1840, Cockington deer park

Carts and carriages ambled into Cockington's deer park early on what promised to be a bright but chilly Monday morning. Vendor booths, some already erected the Saturday prior while others were still under construction, were lined up on both sides of the green space that had been the home of the village fairs for decades.

Meanwhile, at one end of the green, the Baker brothers finished their work on building the stage. Posts had been erected on either side, and a rope had been strung from the top of one to the other. A few minutes later, the curtain Mr. Coulsden had kept on hand from prior year's fairs was hung from the rope and pulled closed so the stage was hidden from view.

On the opposite side of the green, pens had been built for lambs, and nearby, trestles had been set up for displaying the early vegetables and the baked goods.

"There are already more booths set up than there were last year," Mrs. Baker remarked from where she was arranging vegetables on a trestle. She was writing names on small chips of wood and placing them behind each of the entries.

"It's that Lady Wilson contest," Mrs. Stafford remarked. "People are so curious as to who the baronet will choose," she added, waving to the Baker boys as they approached from the stage.

"I feared we wouldn't see such a good turnout when Sir Adam announced no entrants from Torquay would be allowed, but I think you are right. Curiosity will have everyone from Cockington, Livermead and even a few from Torquay coming out for the fair," Mrs. Baker stated.

"The entertainers are here," one of the Baker brothers said as he approached his mother. "They want to know where they should set up."

"Entertainers?" Mrs. Stafford asked in confusion.

"The comedy troupe. Jugglers, fire breathers, jesters," Billy, one of the brothers, clarified. "Said they'd heard about the fair and thought to make some blunt from collecting tips."

Bobby, the other brother, leaned in and said, "One of them is a sword swallower." He put both his hands to his neck and pretended to strangle himself.

"Bobby," Mrs. Baker scolded.

"They can use the stage until the contest starts," Mrs. Stafford said as she surveyed the growing number of vendors arriving from every direction. Vehicles already lined the single lane through town. "As long as they promise not to set fire to the stage, they can use it until noon."

"Is that when the contest starts?" Bobby asked. When his mother regarded him with an arched brow, he said, "I might be wantin' to court one of the women who aren't chosen is all."

"Oh, now you're just teasing me," Mrs. Baker accused.

"Got my eye on Kate," Bobby claimed.

"Only 'cause Eloise has her eye on me," Billy countered, nudging his elbow into his brother's ribs.

Her mouth dropping open in shock, their mother looked as if she might faint. "I don't believe either one of you. Now off with you," she said as she made a shooing motion with a chubby hand.

"You don't believe them?" Mrs. Stafford asked as

she saw to labeling some of the baked goods that had been collecting on the next trestle.

"I happen to know that neither Kate nor Eloise plan to enter the contest," Mrs. Baker claimed. "They said they didn't want the humiliation in the event they weren't chosen, and besides, Kate can't read," she explained. Then she leaned in closer and whispered, "Besides that, I don't expect there will be more than one entry in that contest."

Mrs. Stafford blinked. "What are you saying?" She glanced around, as if she feared they would be overheard.

Mrs. Baker shrugged, pretending innocence. "No entrants from Torquay or Livermead are allowed. That just leaves the unmarried women of Cockington, and we both know there's really only one of them if you don't include Kate and Eloise."

"Only one?"

"Mrs. Longburn," Mrs. Baker stated.

Mrs. Stafford scoffed. "But, what about Miss Barrows? The one who runs the boarding house?" she asked as her brows furrowed. "I was sure she would enter."

Mrs. Baker planted her fists on her ample hips. "Weren't you at the Sunday service yesterday?" she asked, angling her head to one side as if she was challenging her friend.

"You know I was," Mrs. Stafford replied, her bosom thrust out as if she were preparing to do battle.

"Didn't pay any mind to the sermon, though, did you?" Mrs. Baker accused.

"Of course I didn't," Mrs. Stafford admitted. "I was too busy thinking about the fair."

Mrs. Baker scoffed. "Well, if you *had* been paying attention, then you would know that Miss Barrows is married to Reverend Trayfor. Has been for *twelve years*."

Looking as if she'd been slapped across the face, Mrs. Stafford blinked several times. "Married? So… he's not having an illicit *affaire*?" she whispered hoarsely, her disappointment evident.

"Well, not with his wife," Mrs. Baker reasoned before a smile appeared. "I just love a parson with a sense of humor, don't you?" Her eyes widened as she glanced around the deer park grounds. "Oh, my. It's growing crowded."

"Another lamb was just delivered," Bobby called out.

"We'll need more pens," Mrs. Baker said before she turned to Billy and waved him over. "Add some dividers inside the lamb pens," she ordered when he joined her.

"Yes, ma'am." The two overgrown boys hurried off.

Even if there wasn't a fair scheduled, this would have been a regular market day. With the fair, more vendors, fishmongers, and farmers than usual poured into the small village from the Devonshire countryside.

"Any sign of the baronet?" Mrs. Stafford asked, looking up from writing out labels.

Mrs. Baker glanced up from the table of vegetables and gasped. Carriages, gigs, carts, a town coach or two, and teams of horses clogged the only road near the deer park. "Hard to tell," she replied with a satisfied grin. "It seems, my dear Mrs. Stafford, that our little village fair is going to be a resounding success."

eanwhile, back at Wilson Hall
Having just finished his breakfast, Sir Adam was still reading the latest *Torquay Chronicle* when Harris appeared on the threshold, Penelope at his side.

"Good morning, Poppet. Have you already had your breakfast?" Adam asked as he set aside his paper and stood.

Dressed in a pink pinafore over a white dress and

stockings, her hair adorned with a pink ribbon, Penelope looked as if she were ready to attend church. "I had breakfast up in the nursery with Mrs. Longburn," she replied, just then remembering to curtsy. "But she had to leave."

Adam blinked as he bent to take her hand in his. "Leave?" he repeated. His gaze went to Harris, who cleared his throat.

"Mrs. Longburn left a while ago, sir. Said she was needed to help with setting up the fair."

"Hmph," Adam replied. "Did she take the coach?"

Harris cleared his throat. "She walked, sir. She was carrying her valise. Although Mr. Smithton offered to take her, she said you would require the coach when you and Miss Penelope decided to go to the fair."

Adam gave a start. "Her valise?" he questioned, his chest suddenly contracting at the thought Charlotte was leaving his household.

"She was on foot, sir," Harris said, as if he knew what his master was thinking. "Mr. Coulsden took Mrs. McNulty and most of the staff earlier this morning. It is a market day, sir."

Still concerned that Charlotte had taken a valise with her, Adam glanced down at his daughter. "Well, I suppose we should be going then," he said before he kissed the back of his daughter's hand. "You look like you're ready to be the perfect hostess."

She smiled, her lack of front teeth making her appear almost comical. "I am, Father."

"It's a bit chilly out now, sir, but I expect it will warm up before noon."

Adam furrowed a brow. "What happens at noon?"

Harris nearly rolled his eyes. "The Lady Wilson contest, sir. You're expected to choose a wife."

Not even trying to hide his reaction, Adam rolled his eyes. "Oh, that," he murmured. "I suppose it's too late to cancel it?"

"But you can't cancel it, Father," Penelope said in a quiet voice, one of her slippered feet stomping the floor. "I'm hosting it, remember?"

Adam winced. "Of course, Poppet. Come, let's get our coats," he said as he gave his butler a look that might have been fright.

When the two were garbed for the cooler weather, they joined Mr. Smithton and William at the coach and were soon on their way to the Cockington deer park.

CHAPTER 22
A PARSON'S WIFE PROVES
PRICELESS

*M*eanwhile, *at the Barrow's boarding house*

"You're behaving like a Nervous Nellie," Barbara Trayfor accused as she helped Charlotte step into a sapphire ballgown.

"That's because I *am* nervous," Charlotte replied in a plaintive voice. "This was a terrible idea. What was I thinking?"

"That you wish to marry Sir Adam," Barbara replied, ignoring Charlotte's quelling glance. "It's a gorgeous gown. It must have cost a fortune," she added as she did up the last of the jet fastenings in the back.

"Four months' wages," Charlotte admitted, "but I still have my inheritance from Father and some from Mr. Longburn."

Barbara's eyes widened. "Where did you even find it?"

"Madame Josephine's in Torquay," Charlotte replied as she stepped into a pair of black slippers.

"Oh, the shop where the fight broke out," Barbara said with a grin. "Were you there during the infamous altercation?"

Charlotte stiffened. "Why did you say it like that?" she asked in a whisper.

Barbara dipped her head. "I may have heard something, is all," she replied.

"What did you hear? Please tell me."

The parson's wife pretended to adjust the fall of the silk skirt before she said, "Apparently there were no scuffles." When Charlotte's mouth dropped open in shock, she added, "It was all an elaborate ruse to be sure no one from Torquay could enter the contest."

"The fight over the gowns didn't really happen?" Charlotte asked in disbelief. She had read the article in the *Torquay Chronicle*. The constable had been quoted. The shopkeeper had been mentioned by name. "Are you saying the article was… was made up?"

"All fiction," Barbara said with a slight shrug.

"But... why?" Charlotte asked in dismay.

Barbara angled her head to one side. "Don't you want to be the only one who enters the contest?"

Charlotte inhaled to answer but drew her brows together in suspicion. "What are you saying?"

Crossing her arms, Barbara walked around Charlotte, pretending to assess the gown before she said, "There are many in this village who are of the same mind as you, Lottie. They did what they thought was necessary to ensure *you* will be the only one on that stage."

Charlotte scoffed at the same time gratitude filled her chest. "They?"

Barbara shrugged. "Sir Adam's servants, my husband, Kate and Eloise, Mr. Coulsden, Mrs. Baker," she ticked off on one hand. "They all want to see you married to him. So you can be Miss Penelope's mother."

Tears sprang to Charlotte's eyes. "Oh," she murmured softly.

"Oh, no, no, no," Barbara said in alarm. "There will be no tears. At least, not yet. You cannot go up on that stage with red-rimmed eyes," she said as she shoved a hanky into Charlotte's hand.

Dabbing at the corners of her eyes, Charlotte nodded and dared a glance in the mirror over Barbara's dressing table. "You're all so kind," she whispered. "So I suppose I had best get on with it." She sniffled. "What should I do with my hair?"

"I'll see to that," Barbara said as she motioned for Charlotte to take a seat. "Ever since Mr. Trayfor told me about Sir Adam's contest, I just knew you would have to enter," she claimed as she removed the few pins that held up Charlotte's hair.

"Why did you think that?"

"You're too young to spend the rest of your life a widow, and that Wilson girl needs a mother," Barbara said as she brushed Charlotte's hair. "Now, I admit that I only recently met the baronet—and only briefly—but my husband seems to think he just needs a slight push in your direction, and he'll take you to wife."

"A slight push?" Charlotte asked as she watched Barbara pin up her hair as if she'd done it a hundred times. "This contest is more like a very hard shove to ensure a collision."

"Not all collisions have poor results," Barbara remarked.

Charlotte couldn't help but grin at hearing Barbara's comments. "I used to dream about being married to him," she admitted, the first time she had put voice to the words.

Barbara stared at Charlotte's reflection in the mirror, her eyes wide. "Used to?" she repeated. "When was this?"

"Before he married my best friend."

Barbara paused the hand that was about to secure a pin into place. "How long have you *known* him?" she asked in surprise.

"Oh, since before the first year of finishing school in London," Charlotte replied. "Ten, eleven years ago? He and Alice weren't yet married, of course, but it was evident they would one day wed. They were in love, you see."

Staring at the widow a moment too long, Barbara finally resumed working on her hair. "It sounds as if you were in love with him, too."

Charlotte scoffed. "Can a person love someone at the same time they despise them with all their being?" She allowed a shrug when she saw Barbara's look of confusion in the mirror. "For I recall despising him that much. He took my best friend from me. In more ways than one."

Rolling her eyes, Barbara sighed. "I would have thought a woman who has been married would know that, yes, you can despise and love a man all at the same time. Gad, I've certainly been guilty of it more than once since I wed Mr. Trayfor."

Charlotte turned around and stared at Barbara. "You jest."

"I do not," the parson's wife countered. "I love Michael. I have since the day he took me from the life of a lady's maid in a minor aristocrat's townhouse in London and made me his wife."

Understanding dawned on Charlotte's face. "So that's how you know how to style hair," she murmured.

"But with his last calling—when he went off to Cornwall without me—I was fit to be tied. Left me in our apartments in his parents' home in Westminster."

"Cornwall?" Charlotte repeated, just then remembering the parson had mentioned his prior post when he had first arrived in Cockington. "As I recall, he didn't mention the name of the town."

"Some mining community on the coast," Barbara said. "He claimed it was all men and that the parsonage wasn't fit for a human to live in."

"Well, it sounds as if he was protecting you from a poor living situation," Charlotte argued, understanding the parson's point of review.

"He didn't ask me for my opinion, though. He just decided for me," Barbara replied in a huff. "I could have made that parsonage fit for us to live in. Instead, I had to stay behind. When my aunt, Mrs. Barrows, died and I inherited this place, I moved here the first chance I got."

Charlotte's eyes rounded, remembering how long Barbara had been running the boarding house. "Oh, no. And then Longburn got the position here," she reasoned before she winced. "I am so sorry. It was not my idea to ever marry him. The only reason I ended up here in Cockington was because..." She allowed the thought to trail off.

Barbara angled her head to one side. "That little girl? Or her father?" she guessed. "Both?"

Charlotte inhaled softly. "I made a promise to Alice, but I never imagined my father had other ideas. That Longburn had decided to return to the home of his birth. That Sir Adam would be living so close to the village," she claimed. She had known, though. It was why she had begged her father to retire in Devonshire.

"So, a marriage of convenience to a parson," Barbara reasoned as she pinned up another lock of hair.

"Well, not for me certainly. I kept thinking Sir Adam would be in search of a new wife. A mother for Penelope. That I had arrived at the perfect time to fill both positions." Tears collected in the corners of her eyes. "And in less than a month's time, it all went so wrong."

"Oh, no, no, no, no," Barbara said as she plucked the hanky from Charlotte's hand and held it to her cheek. "Remember, there will be no tears on this day. How can you hope to gain a marriage proposal with red-rimmed eyes?"

Charlotte sniffled. "You're doing a remarkable job

on my hair. You do realize that once women know you're capable of such artistry, you'll be doing every-one's hair?"

Barbara's eyes rounded. "Ah, now there's an idea," she murmured. "I've been thinking of selling the boarding house so Michael and I can move into the parsonage, but I would miss the income from this place." She stuck another pin into Charlotte's red hair and stepped back. "I could do hair. For special events, like those parties they have over in Torquay," she added. "Well, Mrs. Longburn, I do believe you're ready. Did you bring a mantle to wear over the gown?"

Charlotte pulled the black cloak from her valise, the garment purchased after Longburn had died as part of her mourning clothes. "I did. I don't want anyone seeing this gown until Miss Penelope announces me," she said as she pulled it on and secured the tie at the neck.

"I don't know about you, but I'm rather excited," Barbara said. "Can't say I've ever felt that way about a village fair before." Her gaze moved to one of the bedchamber's windows. "Oh, my. It seems the fair is attracting more than the usual attendees," she murmured.

Charlotte hurried to the window and stared out. Carriages lined the lane on both sides, and a number of people were on foot, headed in the direction of the deer park. "Noon cannot come soon enough," she murmured.

"Oh, noon is it?" Barbara teased. "I'll be there. Now off with you. I still have to clean a room or two."

"Thank you," Charlotte said as she took Barbara's hand and squeezed it.

"You can thank me after he proposes. And make sure he kisses you."

Charlotte's eyes rounded. "He has to choose me first."

Barbara scoffed. "Well, that won't be hard."

"Why do you say it like that?"

"Aren't you going to be the only one in the contest?" Barbara reminded her.

Managing not to appear too guilty, Charlotte pulled the hood of her mantle over her hair and took her leave of the boarding house.

CHAPTER 23
THE BIG REVEAL

ockington Village Fair, late morning

After stepping down from the traveling coach, Sir Adam was forced to stay close to the carriage given the foot traffic that passed by. He turned and lifted Penelope down from the equipage, gripping her hand lest they get separated in the crowd.

He looked up to find Mr. Smithton grinning before the driver asked, "Have you ever seen so many people in the village, sir?"

"I have not," Adam replied, deciding it best he simply lift Penelope onto his shoulders. "Hang on, Poppet. You're going for a ride," he warned as he turned her around and placed his hands beneath her arms. She giggled in delight as she was hoisted into the air and then ended up on his shoulders.

"I can see everything, Father," she said in delight, her hands gripping the sides of his head beneath the brim of his hat.

"Good, because you're going to have to give me directions," he said as he merged into the line of people making their way from carriages that were parked farther down the lane.

"Are we going to be late?" Penelope asked in worry.

Adam opened his pocket watch. "We still have fifteen minutes," he said, wincing at the thought that in less than a half-hour, he would be choosing his next wife. "Can you see the stage?"

"Oh, yes, Father. There's a man juggling on it, though." She gasped. "And another who just swallowed a sword."

Adam frowned, wondering if she was exaggerating "Which way?"

Penelope leaned down and used a pudgy finger to point toward the stage. The crowd in which they walked seemed to be heading in the same direction, although a few people paused at vendor booths or stopped to admire the huge herd of bleating lambs that were secured in a line of pens that was as long as the field was wide.

"I had no idea we had this many lambs in all of

Devonshire," he murmured.

A huge crowd had gathered in front of the stage to watch the jesters and jugglers. When the sword swallower lit his sword on fire, a gasp went up through the audience. He lowered it into his mouth, the flames appearing to burn his face before they disappeared.

"We kindly accept your contributions," a hawker called out as he passed a basket containing a variety of coins while he managed to juggle two balls with one hand.

Adam fished in his pocket for a coin and tossed it in the basket. Upon seeing him, the hawker's eyes widened. "You wouldn't happen to be the poor sod, Sir Adam, who's supposed to pick a wife today, would you?"

Grimacing, Adam said, "I am indeed that poor sod."

The hawker blinked, as if he'd asked the question of every other man in the audience and expected a denial. "We're almost finished with the show, sir," the hawker said. He looked up and grinned at Penelope. "And I take it you're the hostess for the Lady Wilson contest?"

"I am," Penelope replied, grinning in delight.

"Ah, I've found you. I'm Puck. I'll introduce you when it's time. What should I call you?"

"Miss Penelope," she said proudly. "And we have to

make certain the curtain is closed. To hide all the ladies."

Puck darted a quick glance at Adam before he acknowledged Penelope's comment. "I'll see to it right now, miss, but you'll be wanting your horse here to make his way to the stage right quick."

Penelope giggled. "He's not my horse. He's my father," she said before she giggled again.

Puck gave Adam a wink and hurried off through the crowd while Adam looked for an easier path toward the stage.

"Do you see anyone you know?" Adam asked as they skirted the audience. "Do you see Mrs. Long-burn?" But Penelope was enjoying the attention as they made their way, waving and greeting villagers she recognized. The Coulsden brothers waved, as did Connors, the footman, Mrs. McNulty, and the Trayfors.

By the time Adam arrived at the edge of the stage, the sword swallower had taken his final bow, and the jester's last bawdy joke had the audience groaning.

A few people broke off from the crowd to visit booths. Others wandered off to find food and drink. Puck, dressed in a jester costume of several colors of silk, jumped onto the stage and raised his arms.

"People of Cockington, we are done. We promise," he shouted. A round of titters and laughter could be heard in response. "However, that also means the time has come," he called out. The murmuring died down among those closest to the stage. "Or rather, almost. We have five minutes to wait." He pretended impatience, which drew another round of laughter. "Sir Adam Wilson, fifth baronet of Cockington, will on this day choose from among the eligible women of Cockington, a wife. If you are such a woman, which means you must be unmarried and young enough to abide having children with the poor sod, then I suggest you make your way onto the stage." When one of the female jugglers joined him on the stage and grinned, he added, "Behind the curtain." She quickly disappeared behind the curtain but then reappeared at the other end of the stage to a chorus of laughter.

As Adam lowered Penelope to the stage, applause broke out. She quickly set her skirts to rights and then straightened, nearly at eye level with her father as he winced.

"You look like a poor sod," Penelope said as a blonde brow furrowed.

"I feel like one," Adam admitted. From the edge of where the curtain met the side posts, he saw movement and realized women had probably begun gathering on the stage. "Do you know what to do?"

She nodded. "There will be one you like, Father. I promise."

"There had better be," Adam murmured. "I'll be right over here," he said as he stepped back to the side of the stage. Given how the crowd seemed to move about, he did a quick glance around. When he was sure he wasn't being watched, he ducked behind the curtain and blinked.

Only one woman stood in the middle of the stage. Dressed in a hooded black mantel and facing the curtain that hid her from the crowd, she could have been anyone.

Adam climbed onto the stage using the two steps at the back, determined to discover her identity before the curtain was pulled open.

At hearing the sound of boot heels on the wood stage, the woman whirled around. "You nearly frightened me to death," she accused. "What are you doing back here? You're supposed to be out..."

Charlotte couldn't finish her sentence. Not when the hood was pushed from her head and her lips were covered by Adam's. The kiss was so unexpected, she couldn't even respond before he pulled away slightly.

"I cannot tell you how relieved I am," he said before he once again kissed her.

Charlotte barely heard the sound of the hawker announcing Miss Penelope's name. She did hear Penelope's voice as she welcomed the crowd. Apparently, Adam did as well, because he had to end the kiss in order to chuckle.

"She's taking this very seriously."

"As she should," Charlotte countered. "She wants a mother." From the other side of the curtain, she heard Penelope explain that her father, the fifth baronet Wilson, would be choosing a wife on this day.

"She wants *you* as her mother," he countered before he kissed her again.

From the other side of the curtain, Penelope continued her recitation. "His new wife will have to be my mother." Her childish voice having finally silenced the crowd, she added, "And she'll have to be my brother's mother, too." This last had a few in the audience tittering.

"And you?" Charlotte whispered. "Do you want me to be the mother of all your children?"

Adam's brows furrowed. "I thought I was making that quite clear," he responded, "but I can try harder." He wrapped an arm around her waist and pulled her against the front of his body.

Heartened that he didn't seem disappointed by the lack of more contestants, Charlotte returned his kiss in full measure. She undid the tie of the mantle and lifted her arms to wrap around his neck, which sent the black wrap fluttering to the stage. At the same moment, Penelope asked that the curtain be opened.

A stunned silence settled over the crowd as the fabric separated. Penelope's gasp, echoed by several in the audience, was following by a giggle and then a plaintive, "Father! You weren't supposed to choose already."

Laughter and a few inappropriate hoots and hollers sounded from the crowd.

Adam gave his daughter an apologetic glance before he stepped back and regarded Charlotte's gown and coiffure. A look of awe settled on his face. "God, you're gorgeous."

Sure she was as red as her hair at having been discovered kissing the baronet in front of such a large audience, Charlotte curtsied to both Adam and the crowd.

Turning his attention to the largest assemblage of people he'd ever seen in Cockington, Adam said, "Good day, everyone. I'd like to introduce you to the only contestant to enter my bride contest," he said in mock despair. The crowd responded with a chorus of surprised gasps and some applause. "I give you the woman who will be my Lady Wilson," Adam called out. "Mrs. Charlotte Longburn."

A few cheers and polite clapping followed the announcement along with some grumbles about the contest being fixed. Within moments, the crowd dissipated and Penelope had joined her father and Charlotte.

Puck stood in front of the stage, his hands on his hips. "Well, that was rather anticlimactic," he complained.

"There was only one woman who entered," Adam said with a shrug.

"She cheated," Puck replied, one of his hands waving through the air before he turned and hurried off to join the rest of his troupe.

When Charlotte didn't put voice to a protest, Adam regarded her with an arched brow. "You're not even going to defend yourself?"

Charlotte lifted her chin. "Against a baseless claim? Never," she replied, barely able to contain her amusement. "Now kind sir, do you think you might escort us off this stage?"

"Gladly," Adam replied as he took hold of Penelope's hand and offered an arm to Charlotte.

CHAPTER 24
PROPOSALS AND PROMISES

few minutes later

Rather than returning to Wilson Hall immediately following the contest, Adam gave into Penelope's request that they stay at the fair. She wanted to see the lambs, and she was intrigued by the variety of goods being sold at the booths.

"Oh, please, Father," she begged. "May we stay?"

Adam exchanged a quick glance with Charlotte, his eyes dark. "You're the one dressed for a London ball," he murmured.

Her mantle draped over one arm, Charlotte demurred. "The lawn is dry, and besides, this gown is almost too short for me."

"I hadn't noticed," he replied, his gaze dropping to

discover her slippered feet could be seen beneath the hem of her gown.

As they made their way from booth to booth, occasionally stopping to buy something, well-wishers called out greetings. Those who had grumbled at the outcome seemed to have left the grounds, for no one directed rude comments at them.

"So when will I have the honor of marrying you two?" Michael Trayfor asked as he and Barbara joined them to admire the early vegetables. Colored ribbons decorated the winning entries.

Charlotte and Adam exchanged quick glances. "Well, since I don't have a special license, I suppose we have to wait a few weeks?" Adam guessed.

"First banns won't be read until Sunday, so, yes, three weeks from today is the earliest I'd be allowed to marry you," Michael agreed. "Mid-May wedding?"

"It will be perfect," Charlotte said. "And enough time to find a gown."

"Where did you get this one?" Adam asked as he fingered the sapphire satin of her skirt.

"Madame Josephine's in Torquay," she replied. "And, no, there weren't any tiffs occurring when I was there."

Adam chuckled just as William Coulsden appeared. "Enough traffic has cleared out that I was able to get the coach pulled up closer, sir," he said. "And best wishes ta ye both."

"Thank you," they replied in unison.

"Glad ta see all our work paid off, sir," William added, winking before he headed back down the lane.

Charlotte blinked. "What did he mean by that?" she asked.

Adam shook his head. "Probably just referring to how well the fair turned out this year. Shall we stop by and see who won ribbons in the baked goods competition?"

Giving him a suspicious glance, Charlotte said, "All right."

When the only people left on the deer park grounds were the two matronly organizers and the Baker boys, Adam made his way to them and said, "Congratulations on a most successful fair," he said as he bowed.

"Oh, thank *you*, sir," Mrs. Baker replied, as she curtsied. "I'm quite sure it was the contest that had so many people visiting our fine village."

"Well, that and the lamb contest," Mrs. Stafford said, joining in the conversation. "The Baker boys were building pens all morning to accommodate the huge turnout. Whoever thought there were this many lambs in all of Devonshire?"

"I take it the prize winners have all been notified?" Adam asked.

"Oh, yes," Mrs. Baker answered. "Why, the money you donated for prizes was so generous, sir, and such a surprise. Why, my boy Bobby says he made enough on his winning lamb that he can propose marriage to Miss Kate."

"That's wonderful," Adam replied, unaware the farmer had his eye on the servant girl.

"And Mrs. McNulty's entry in the baked goods competition was a blue ribbon winner. Mr. Coulsden was so excited for her, he kissed her right in front of everyone and God," she claimed.

"That's because he loves her," Penelope piped up, which had Adam chuckling.

"Did he propose marriage?" Charlotte asked, hope in her voice.

Mrs. Stafford shook her head, her lips pinched together before she said, "Poor man."

"Poor sod," Penelope murmured.

"Poppet," Adam said under his breath. He glanced around, wincing at how the lawn of the deer park had been trampled by the crowds.

"Oh, you needn't be concerned, sir," Mrs. Baker said. "It will be right as rain right after the next rain."

At that moment, the slight breeze turned into a wind, and gray clouds rolled in on the horizon.

Adam, Charlotte, and Penelope managed to take cover in the coach before the rain began to fall.

*L*ater that night

By the time she led Penelope up to the nursery after dinner, Charlotte was sure she had heard 'best wishes' from every servant in Wilson Hall. The girl had nearly fallen asleep in her soup but was managing to negotiate the stairs to the third floor without any help when Mrs. Heber appeared to claim her.

"She's had a big day," Charlotte whispered.

"Oh, haven't we all?" Mrs. Heber replied as she lifted the girl into her arms. "I must admit, I was so relieved when you were the only woman on that stage today. I feared there would be some upstart from out-of-town that might have the baronet changing his mind about you."

Charlotte blinked. "Changing his mind?" she repeated.

The nursemaid's eyes widened. "Oh, well, we all knew it was you he wanted to wed. He just a needed a little... *encouragement*, is all."

"Encouragement?" Charlotte prompted.

"Well, we wouldn't have *really* done what we said we was going to do," Mrs. Heber went on. "But he didn't know that."

Charlotte blinked again. "What did you do? Or... or not do?" she asked in alarm.

"Why, we threatened to quit, is all."

"Mrs. Heber!"

"Got his attention, it did. But he knows what's best for him and..." She suddenly straightened. "I'd best get this little lady upstairs and into bed." The nursemaid hurried up the next flight of stairs, leaving Charlotte open-mouthed.

She turned to discover Adam on the landing below, leaning against the railing with his arms crossed over his chest. She angled her head to one side, and a moment of doubt had her saying, "You were bribed into selecting me?"

He chuckled before he climbed the stairs to join her on the third floor. "One cannot bribe a man who has already made the right decision," he replied in a low voice.

A frisson skittered down her spine, and Charlotte inhaled softly. "And what might that decision be?"

Adam gave a start. "To choose you to be my wife, of course."

"Hmm," she murmured. "And yet, I've not heard a proposal."

Furrowing a brow, Adam inhaled and let the air out slowly. "I thought I'd see to that in a more private setting," he whispered as he took her hand and led her down the hall toward her apartment.

"Oh?" Her voice sounded breathy, and Charlotte wondered how long her legs might be able to hold her up. For some reason, they felt wobbly.

"The master suite," he said as he stopped at her door. "Will a half-hour be long enough for you to dress for bed? If not, I can see to your pins," he offered. "I wouldn't wish to ruin your coiffure, but after last night, I know how long your hair is, and I find I wish to see it like that again tonight."

Charlotte inhaled softly, understanding what he intended. He wished for her to share his bed. "I think I can manage," she murmured. Her breaths seemed to come too fast. "But I do need help with my buttons," she said as she turned around.

Adam chuckled as he opened the door to her suite, pulled her into it, and shut the door. Then he reached up and undid each of the jet buttons until the gown sagged from her shoulders. He kissed the bare skin above her chemise as one hand pushed down her sleeve. When her arm was free, he did the same with the other.

"Where exactly is the master suite?" she asked as she turned around in his arms.

"Second floor, beneath this apartment," he whispered before he took her lips with his and kissed her softly.

When he slowly released his hold on her, Charlotte swayed before she said, "Give me forty-five minutes."

She watched as Adam gave a reluctant nod, opened the door, and then quickly made his way back toward the stairs.

Or at least as quickly as he could. His arousal made it difficult to walk.

CHAPTER 25
A TIMID MAN IS EMBOLDENED

*M*eanwhile, in the kitchen of Wilson Hall

Once the horses were unhitched, brushed, and fed, William entered the kitchen in search of a late dinner. Although he had supped on a meat pie from the fair earlier that afternoon and helped himself to several Dutch biscuits before tending to the horses, he was starving.

His serviette at the trestle at which the servants sat for their meals was still in place, the empty plate surrounded by trays of cheese, bread, and some slices of roast beef.

Smacking his lips, William settled into his chair and helped himself to the hearty fare. About to take his first bite, he couldn't when he realized he wasn't alone.

"I thought I might find you here," Mrs. McNulty said when she entered the kitchen.

William immediately stood. "How do, Mrs. McNulty?" he said as he gave a slight bow. "Have you been in town all this time?" He winced at the thought she might have walked home from the fair in the dark. "I could have brought you back in the gig."

Mrs. McNulty waved a hand. "Goodness no. I've been back most of the day," she claimed as she placed a mug of ale on the table in front of William. She set another on the trestle across from him and then sat down. "Wanted to be sure everything was perfect in the master and mistress suites," she added, lifting a brow to emphasize her point.

William reddened with embarrassment. "You don't think they're... well, I mean, seein' as how they cannot be wed for a few weeks—"

"He's a widower. She's a widow. Don't be thinking he's going to wait to claim her as his wife until after the vows are spoken," Mrs. McNulty replied in a whisper. "Would you?"

The groom stared at the housekeeper, not sure what he would do. Sensing a trap, William straightened on the bench seat. "Well, I suppose that all depends," he hedged.

Mrs. McNulty arched a dark brow. "On what?"

"Why, on the lady, of course," he replied.

"Really?" she countered. "How do you mean?"

William realized he wasn't going to be able to wiggle out of a more detailed response and said, "If my lady wants my company in her bed, then I'd be much obliged to accommodate her."

Giving him a prim grin, Mrs. McNulty nodded her understanding. "And if she wishes your company but maybe not in a bed? If you catch my meaning?"

William furrowed a brow, not sure what she meant by 'company not in a bed.' Was she asking him if he would be willing to bed her somewhere other than in her bed?

Before he could answer, Mrs. McNulty tittered. "Oh goodness, Mr. Coulsden. I didn't mean to embarrass you," she claimed.

"Were you asking me if I would accommodate you in another room of the house? Like the library?" he asked in a whisper. "Because I would. Where ever you'd like, actually. Exceptin' for maybe in here, since anyone could walk in on us," he added.

Mrs. McNulty's eyes rounded. "Oh!" She blinked. "Well, that's not exactly what I meant, but I appreciate knowing you'd be willing," she said before she took another drink from her mug of ale.

Even in the dim candlelight, William could see a

blush color her face. Understanding dawned on him. "You meant company as... as in companionship. Someone to talk to," he clarified, barely managing to hide his disappointment. He nearly drained his mug of ale in one gulp.

"Indeed," she replied. She leaned forward and said, "But now that I know you'd be willing to... to *accommodate* me, perhaps we could agree to meet," she suggested, arching one brow.

It was William's turn to blink. "Whenever you'd like," he replied. "Where ever you'd like," he quickly added. "I don't suppose you'd agree to be me wife whilst you're being so agreeable?"

She tittered and sighed. "Maybe in a year or two," she teased. "After I've had a chance to discover the extent of your... *accommodations*," she added.

William grinned and sat back. "Just tell me when and where, Mrs. McNulty, and I'm yours."

The housekeeper grinned and took another sip of her ale. "Finish your dinner, Mr. Coulsden," she said before she stood to leave.

Quick to rise from his seat, William held his breath. "And then?" he prompted.

"The guest bedchamber on the third floor at the end of the hall," she stated. "Not the end where the nursery and servants' quarters are," she quickly added.

Not having ever been in that wing of the third floor, William could only hope it would be apparent. "Very well. I shan't disappoint," he promised.

Mrs. McNulty finished her ale and regarded the groom with a grin. "Of course you won't." With that, she took her leave of the kitchen.

William swallowed and regarded his dinner with renewed interest. Sitting down, he went about consuming everything on his plate.

He would need his strength.

CHAPTER 26
A PAST PROVES
PROBLEMATIC

orty minutes later

Nervous and excited, Charlotte stepped out of her apartments. Dressed in her best night rail with her silk dressing gown wrapped tightly around her body, she padded down the corridor to the stairs, hoping none of the servants were up and about.

When she reached Adam's door, she found it ajar. Pausing a moment, she listened for any indication he was in the room. Feeling like a thief in the night, she slipped in and closed the door. She turned around and allowed her eyes to adjust to the dark before she made her way through the sitting room and to the bedchamber beyond.

"I was beginning to think you weren't coming," Adam said from where he sat on the opposite edge of the bed. His bare back was to her, and Charlotte had a thought he was naked. If she'd been nervous upon entering his suite, she didn't know how to describe her current state. Her heart was pounding so loudly, she was sure he could hear it.

"It hasn't even been forty-five minutes," she said as she crept around the end of the four-poster bed. Her slippered feet seemed to sink into the carpet with her every step, and her gaze swept the dim room. Dark woods and deep blues seemed to swallow the little bit of light provided by a wall-mounted sconce near his side of the bed and a candle lamp on the bedside table.

"There are times it has seemed like an eternity," he countered as he glanced up at her.

Charlotte gave a start when she realized he was, indeed, naked. His arousal, jutting from a nest of dark curls, had her gasping softly. "As it has sometimes been for me," she whispered as she sat next to him.

He lifted a hand to push a lock of hair behind her shoulder. "And yet you married another," he accused.

"Because I had no choice," she said on a huff.

"Didn't you?" he asked in a hoarse whisper.

"I wasn't yet one-and-twenty," she replied. "Father seemed to think it important I be married—for protection—before he died," she reminded him. "You were away from Cockington on some trip to a silk farm, I think. I had no other way out."

"You could have walked away, Charlotte," he argued.

Scoffing, Charlotte stared at him. "A man could have," she countered, growing annoyed by his line of questioning. "A young woman could not." She swallowed, surprised they were speaking so frankly, as if they had known one another for many years. They had in many respects, given their mutual love of Alice. Having read the woman's diary, they now knew intimate details of one another they wouldn't otherwise know.

"Do you have any idea what it was like to see that decrepit man squiring you about town?" Adam asked, his voice sounding strained. "Strutting about like a damned peacock?"

Charlotte stared at him a moment, surprised at the sound of jealousy in his voice. "That's all it was, Adam. He was nothing to me."

Adam suddenly stood and then pulled her up from the bed. She inhaled when he stripped the dressing gown from her body and then pushed her onto the bed. "Nothing?" he repeated as he settled atop her, his engorged cock digging into one muslin-covered thigh.

"Does that mean you will not think of him when we are together?"

Her eyes narrowing, Charlotte said, "I will not think of him ever again. In fact, I would not have thought of him on this day at all but for your talk of him."

Even as his anger seemed to flow over and around her, Charlotte couldn't help how her body responded to his closeness. To his familiar scent. To the weight of his body atop her. To the sensation of his throbbing manhood.

Excitement had the space at the top of her thighs growing damp, her nipples hardening into tight buds.

She nearly cried out when one of his hands pushed up her night rail and pressed on her mons. Moving her free leg aside—he had the other pinned to the bed with his hip—she inhaled sharply when his entire hand slid along the delicate folds protecting her womanhood, his fingers separating them as he pulled his hand away. She inhaled again when one finger brushed over her womanhood, and then she cried out when his thumb pressed it, rubbing it until sharp sensations of pleasure coursed through her lower body.

Before she could catch her breath, he lifted himself from her body and pushed her other knee to the side. Hooking one of his arms under the other knee, he forced it to lift from the bed.

He entered her in one hard thrust, as if he meant to ensure any remnants of Ambrose Longburn were eradicated from her body. Stilling himself, he seemed to struggle to catch his breath before he pulled himself almost entirely from her body.

Charlotte whimpered and held her breath as he thrust into her again, this time more slowly. Not exactly sure what to do, she lifted her other knee to better cradle his body. When she attempted to place her hands on his shoulders—she desperately wished for something to hang onto—he grabbed each wrist in turn and pushed them into the mattress above her head.

With her breasts forced up as they were, he paused to take one of the fabric-covered nipples between his teeth. She gasped when he nearly bit it, jerking to the side in an attempt to free herself from his hold.

He thrust into her again and again, and a low growling groan had her holding her breath as he ceased his movements. A moment later, and he rolled off of her and onto the bed, soft snores soon replacing his labored breathing.

CHAPTER 27
A BAD DREAM

*T*ears pricked the corners of Charlotte's eyes as she turned her head in the pillow. The very last thing she wanted was for Adam to see her cry. She had no idea why he was so angry. Why he seemed so upset with her over her marriage to Ambrose.

Or perhaps he'd been upset because she didn't know what to do. She thought she had done everything she was supposed to, but then, what did she know?

She had never done this before.

"Charlotte?"

The quiet word wasn't said by Adam, who seemed to have fallen asleep as soon as he rolled off her body, but rather by Penelope.

Clutching the bed linens to her chest, Charlotte

raised herself onto an elbow. "What is it? Why are you out of your bed?" she asked in a whisper.

Garbed in her white night rail, Penelope looked as if she, too, was crying. "I had a bad dream." She stepped to the side and furrowed her blonde brows. "Is my father sleeping?"

"He is," Charlotte replied, wincing when she saw that he wasn't even covered. She slid her hand around the counterpane in an effort to find her dressing gown. Pulling the garment around her shoulders, she slipped from the bed and lifted the young girl into her arms.

The scents of Adam surrounded her—the citrus laundry soap and amber cologne—and she realized too late she had pulled on his silk banyan.

"You smell like Father," the girl whispered.

"You like it, though, don't you?" Charlotte murmured with a wan grin, giving the girl a kiss on the cheek as she hurried from the bedchamber. With Penelope's bottom resting on her hip and her arms wrapped around her neck, Charlotte was struck by how natural it was to carry the young girl. As if she had done it a hundred times.

She could only hope she would do so even more in the future. After hearing Adam's comments—his accusations—she didn't know if she'd ever be welcomed in his bed—or in his house. He hadn't even proposed marriage and yet she had allowed him to thoroughly ruin her.

"Will you stay with me until I fall asleep?" Penelope asked as Charlotte climbed the stairs to the third floor. "I'm afraid of the bad dream."

"Of course, darling," Charlotte said as she entered the nursery. She moved to the rocking chair in the corner and settled into it.

"Why were you sleeping in Father's bed?"

Charlotte adjusted Penelope so she was seated on her lap. "Because... I'm to be his wife," she whispered as she fought off the urge to weep.

For the first time since he had kissed her on the stage at noon, Charlotte felt the true impact of the words. Whether she liked it or not—whether *he* liked it or not—they were to be married. It was too late to back out now.

"So, you'll be my mother now?"

"Yes, darling. I am your mother now." A sense of calm settled over Charlotte as she gently rocked in the chair. When the silence was about to overwhelm her, she said, "I promised your real mother I would see to it you could read."

Penelope stiffened in her hold. "You knew my mother? The one who gave birth to me?"

Charlotte kissed the side of Penelope's head as she

cradled her. "Oh, yes. Alice was my very best friend when I lived in London," she replied, tears once again threatening. "I miss her very much."

Penelope's head rested into the small of Charlotte's shoulder, and she said, "I do, too."

"She loved you so much," Charlotte whispered, struggling to suppress a sob. Even before she had finished the comment, she knew Penelope was sound asleep. A moment later, she joined the girl in a fitful slumber.

CHAPTER 28
A GROOM ACCOMMODATES

*M*eanwhile, *in another wing of Wilson Hall*

Using the servants stairs at the back of the house, William climbed to the third floor and was about to make his way down the corridor when he sensed someone was nearby.

Stepping back into the stairwell, he peeked around the corner and frowned as he watched Mrs. Longburn walking in his direction. Miss Penelope was perched on her hip, her arms wrapped around the governess' neck. The youngster was murmuring something about her bad dream when Mrs. Longburn disappeared through an open door.

The nursery, William realized. Unfortunately, Mrs.

Longburn didn't close the door behind her, and William was forced stay where he was when she didn't leave the room.

He listened intently but was unable to make out any words in the murmurs and whispers between the governess and her charge. It wasn't long before William realized the conversation had ended.

Waiting a few more minutes before he dared step into the corridor, William slid along the wall, daring a glance into the nursery. Despite the darkness, he could see that Mrs. Longburn had settled into a chair with Miss Penelope snuggled against her. From the soft breathing he could hear, he realized they were both asleep.

He stood and watched the two for a moment. From what Mrs. McNulty had implied—that Sir Adam would be bedding his intended on this night—William wondered how she could have been so wrong.

Perhaps Mrs. Longburn insisted on marrying before she would share a bed with Sir Adam. Or perhaps the baronet was simply content to wait until the vows had been said.

Realizing he would be discovered if Mrs. Longburn awoke, William hurried on down the corridor to the end. He found one door slightly ajar, a faint light lining the opening.

He knocked softly before stepping into the guest bedchamber. Quietly shutting the door behind him, he winced when he realized it didn't have a lock.

"I wondered if you got lost," Mrs. McNulty teased in a hoarse whisper.

William turned around to find the housekeeper wearing nothing but her shift. He inhaled softly. "No, but I was detained when Mrs. Longburn carried Miss Penelope into the nursery," he replied. He glanced at the bed. The counterpane and bed linens had been pulled down, and the drapes were closed.

"That's odd," she replied, moving to stand in front of William. She reached up to undo the knot at his neck.

"Girl had a bad dream," he murmured. "And seein' as she obviously went to Mrs. Longburn instead of her father, it seems the baronet isn't claimin' his bride on this night."

Mrs. McNulty paused in unwrapping the neckcloth from around his neck. "You sound disappointed," she murmured.

William furrowed his brows. "Not disappointed," he replied as he took her hands in his. He raised them to his lips, kissing the backs of them before turning them over to kiss her palms. "But it has me thinking."

Her eyes rounding at his show of affection, Mrs.

McNulty stared at him as if seeing him for the first time. "Thinking about what?" she asked.

"Marriage. And how much I want to be married to you," he replied. "I have for some time," he added.

She dipped her head. "I know."

He gasped. "You do?"

She gave him a quelling glance. "Everyone in Cockington knows," she said on a sigh.

He inhaled to put voice to a protest but quickly shut his mouth. "I thought it was only my brother who knew," he murmured.

"It's nothing to be ashamed of," Mrs. McNulty said, extracting her hands from his so she could undo his waistcoat buttons.

"Oh, I'm not ashamed," he responded. After a pause, he added, "Other than by how long it's taken for me ta put voice to me intentions towards you."

She pushed the waistcoat from his shoulders. "Do you know why it was I spoke with you whilst you were having your dinner this evening?" she asked as she gathered fistfuls of his linen shirt and pulled up on them.

"Because you didn't have anything better to do?" he guessed, finally helping her with removing his shirt from his body.

Swallowing at the sight of the groom's naked chest,

Mrs. McNulty blinked. She stared at the expanse of crisp curls and skin and muscled torso for a moment before she lifted her gaze up to his. "Because I grew tired of waiting, Mr. Coulsden."

"You can call me William."

"I'm not getting any younger, and neither are you," she scolded as her hand hovered over his chest. "You can call me Margaret," she added.

William took her hand and pressed it over his heart. "You've been here a long time, Margaret," he murmured. "Before tonight, you never gave me the slightest hint you might want me." He leaned over and pressed a kiss on her forehead. "What happened to change that?"

Margaret inhaled softly. "All the excitement over the bride contest, I suppose," she whispered. "I was married once, you know. A long time ago."

He shook his head. "I don't remember that," he said.

"Married just before my Robert sailed over to the Continent. He died when his ship was hit by the French," she whispered. "Two months."

William wrapped his arms around her and pulled her against his body. "I am very sorry for your loss."

"Oh, don't be," she replied. "He was an arse."

Releasing her so he could look her in the eye, William gave a start. "Do you mean that?"

She scoffed. "He only married me to get in my skirts," she groused.

"That's not why I want to marry you," William stated.

Margaret inhaled softy and then nodded. "I know," she replied. "You're an honorable man, William Coulsden."

"So... you'll marry me?" he asked, once again pulling her close. "'Cuz I'm not going to... to accommodate you if you're not."

She angled her head, her gaze softening when their eyes once again met. "I told you I would," she whispered.

Letting out a strangled cry when William lifted her into his arms and then placed her onto the bed, Margaret watched in awe as he removed his boots and trousers and smalls in only a few seconds.

When he stood regarding her from the side of the bed, his manhood jutting out in front of him as if in search of its target, Margaret gasped. "Well, it looks as if you'll be accommodating me right quick," she murmured.

"Not right quick," he countered before he climbed onto the bed next to her.

"No?" she whispered.

He shook his head. "I'd like to take my time," he said as his eyes darkened. His lips covered hers, and Margaret relaxed back onto the bed.

Neither one returned to their quarters until the following morning.

CHAPTER 29
AFTERMATH

*S*tartled from his brief nap, Adam reached out with a hand. He was sure he hadn't ended up too far from Charlotte when he rolled from her soft body. He winced when he remembered what he had said to her just before he'd had his way with her. When he remembered her look of confusion and hurt.

Sitting up, he found he wasn't too surprised she was no longer in his bed. He couldn't blame her for escaping to the mistress chamber. He had been an ass. A brute.

Why he had thought it necessary to put voice to such uncharitable comments about Charlotte and the parson, he didn't know. He hadn't realized how much he'd been bothered by their union until after he had left her in her apartment earlier that evening.

The forty minutes he'd been entirely alone—the first since breakfast that morning—had his mind whirling with what his servants had attempted—a coup to quit his service—along with what he had done to further ensure Charlotte would be the only woman on the stage at the Lady Wilson contest.

The prize monies he had offered for the other contests at the fair were essentially bribes to ensure a larger than usual turnout for the baked goods, vegetables, and lambs. The article in the *Torquay Chronicle*... well, he almost wished *he* had been the one to come up with the idea. His cousins had seen to it, though, bless their hearts. They seemed to believe they had as much at stake in the outcome of the Lady Wilson contest as they'd had when they were lads.

The damned contest.

Feeling around for his banyan, Adam discovered it was missing. Turning up the flame on the bedside lamp, he winced at the sudden light, his gaze forced away and across the bed linens. Although they had been a pristine white when turned down earlier that evening, they were no longer.

He stared at the bloodstain that now marred the expanse of white, confusion furrowing his brow.

There had been a similar bloodstain the night after he had first bedded Alice, proof of her virtue and a reminder that he was honor-bound to wed her. Marrying Alice had always been his intention, though. He loved her. He had for all the years they had known one another in London.

Charlotte was a widow, though. The same age as Alice, but married for at least three years to the old parson. Surely the man would have bedded her every chance he could get.

What man wouldn't want those long legs wrapped around their thighs? That red hair splayed over their pillows? The round breasts beneath their lips?

Even now, the memory of her in his bed had his cock hardening.

Remembering Charlotte's behavior only the hour before, Adam cursed softly, realization and understanding washing over him in a rush.

Despite his reaction to the ribbing he had received from the crass men in the village, Reverend Longburn hadn't bedded Charlotte every chance he could get. He probably hadn't bedded her at all, which meant she had been left a virgin bride.

Pulling on the only dressing gown he could find —from the faint scent of honeysuckle, he knew it was Charlotte's—he lifted the lamp from the bedside table. One of Penelope's soft toys, a doll he had bought for her in Darlington, appeared in the pool of light on the carpet, and he bent to pick it up.

He stared at it a moment, sure it was the one she slept with every night. If so, why was it here and not in the nursery?

Alarm had Adam padding through the dressing room and into the mistress suite. Finding the bed still made and no sign of Charlotte, he hurried up to the third floor and into the nursery.

He stopped short on the threshold, struck by the sight of his betrothed wrapped in his banyan, asleep with her head resting atop his daughter's.

Guilt, love, regret, and determination swept through him all at once as he moved to the rocking chair. He placed a kiss on Charlotte's forehead and then scooped his daughter into his arms.

Charlotte awakened with a start, her slight inhalation of breath loud in the quiet nursery.

"Shh," he managed as he placed Penelope on her bed and covered her with the bed linens and blanket. He tucked the toy under the top edge of the linens.

"She had a bad dream," Charlotte whispered when she joined him at the side of the bed.

"You must have as well, when you realized what a detestable man you've agreed to marry," he said, pulling her against his body.

"What?"

"Not here," he said as he lifted her into his arms and carried her from the nursery.

"What are you doing?" Charlotte asked in a whisper. She was forced to wrap her arms around his neck, fearing if she didn't, she might end up on the floor.

"I'm taking you back to bed. Our bed. Where I'm going to apologize profusely for my behavior earlier this evening, and you're going to explain to me how it is you were still a virgin despite being married for three years."

Charlotte inhaled softly. "It was that obvious? I was that bad?" she asked as she grimaced.

Adam scoffed as he descended the stairs. "You had every right to be given your inexperience," he countered. "You should have told me. I cannot tell you how jealous I was of Longburn, thinking he was bedding you every night."

Furrowing a brow, Charlotte huffed. "I suppose Alice was the perfect bedmate on *your* wedding night," she accused, well aware Adam had taken his wife's virtue well before they were married. When she saw the look of hurt cross Adam's face, she added, "I apologize. That's was unkind of me."

Adam sighed. "Alice was perfect on our wedding night because... because I'd already taken her virtue," he admitted as he entered the master suite and lowered her to the bed. "I'd had the pleasure of her body many times before our wedding day, in fact."

"As was your right, I suppose," Charlotte murmured, deciding not to admit what Alice had told her. What betrothed young lady hadn't been ruined before her wedding day? There was a reason first babes always seemed to arrive well before a couple had been wed nine months.

"But you knew that," he added, ignoring her comment as he lifted a hip and sat on the edge of the bed.

Charlotte grimaced, realizing Alice must have told Adam everything she had shared with Charlotte. "I did. Alice was my best friend. She told me everything. And when she died, I... I blamed you."

Adam gave a start. "Me?"

"You got a child on her. A child that cost her her life."

Adam winced. "Believe me when I tell you I have felt nothing but guilt ever since. But whatever you do, *please* do not blame her death on Penelope," he whispered.

Shocked he would think her capable, Charlotte lifted a hand to the side of his head. "Oh, Adam, I do not. Believe *me* when I say that I love that girl as if she were my own. I had to promise Alice that I would, and I'm happy... I'm *honored* to do so," she said in a rush. When she was finished, she sighed and then admitted, "I wanted to marry you because of her."

Adam inhaled slowly at hearing her confession. Let out the breath even slower as he parsed her words. "And now you probably hate me," he whispered.

"I do not," she countered, her eyes rounding. "I'll have you know..." She clamped her lips shut.

Angling his head to one side, Adam prompted, "Know what?"

Her shoulders slumping in his oversized banyan, Charlotte sighed and said, "I almost ran away when Father told me I was to marry the parson."

Adam furrowed a dark brow. "So... you really didn't want to marry him?"

Charlotte's eyes rounded. "Of course not. He was old. I don't think he even wanted a wife, except to show off in front of the other old men," she claimed. "Besides, I wanted you."

Adam scoffed. "You did?"

She nodded. "I wanted to keep my promise to Alice and... well... she had already told me so much about you, and how you were a good man, and a good husband, and a good..." She stopped speaking as her cheeks flamed with color.

"Go on," he urged, curious as to what his late wife had shared with Charlotte.

"A good lover," she whispered.

Straightening, Adam felt the familiar pang of loss every time he thought of Alice, but this time, it was accompanied by a sense of relief.

Alice had wanted him to marry Charlotte.

Alice had wanted Charlotte to see to their child if something had happened to her, and she had.

"Well, I still need to prove that to you, and I shall," he vowed. "But first, I think we must agree to something."

Charlotte straightened on the bed. "Agree to what?"

Adam swallowed, surprised that his throat hadn't closed as it usually did when he thought of his late wife. "Alice is no longer alive. I know that in my heart and in my bones. Nothing we do or say will bring her back."

"I understand," Charlotte murmured. "But we can keep the memory of her alive. For Penelope."

He nodded. "Agreed. But not at the expense of our marriage," he whispered.

Charlotte angled her head to one side. "I didn't think you would still wish to—"

"I'm not going to marry you simply to gain a mother for Penelope," he interrupted. "I'm going to marry you because... because she wanted *you* to be Penelope's mother."

Charlotte grimaced, curious if he had only just learned of Alice's secret from having read the diary. "How long have you known that?"

He sighed. "Those boxes in the attic? As you know, they held far more than just my grandfather's documents," he murmured. "Far more than just her diary and her jewel box."

Charlotte gasped. "What else?"

Adam dipped his head. "Letters," he stated. "I didn't read all of them, but, yes, I learned what she made you promise."

Hearing his admission had Charlotte feeling vulnerable, as if he knew all her secrets. "And the contest? Why did you go through with it if—?"

"Curiosity, I suppose," he interrupted with a smirk. "I wanted to discover if you wished to be my wife," he admitted. "That you would go to such trouble—and that the staff would as well—so you would be the only entrant merely assured me you did."

Charlotte's face colored before she asked, "And if I hadn't entered the contest?"

He winced. "Well, I wouldn't have married Eloise or Kate, if that's what you're asking," he teased. "Especially since I happen to know who they will be marrying," he added with a smirk. When he noted Charlotte's look of confusion, he said, "The Baker boys. My tenant farmers."

"Oh, of course," Charlotte said as she straightened.

Sobering, Adam said, "If you hadn't entered the contest, I might have had to move to a monastery. Because *I* want you to be my wife."

Her mouth rounding in an 'O,' Charlotte stared at him. "Oh, Adam," she breathed. She leaned forward and placed a hand on the side of his cheek. She kissed him, reveling in how their mouths met and fit perfectly, in how his tongue teased hers before the tip of it brushed her teeth.

When he finally pulled away, he said, "Stay right there." He stood from the bed and moved to the pitcher and bowl of water on the dressing table.

Pouring some water into the bowl, he wet a cloth and wrung it out. When he returned to the bed, he found Charlotte staring at him with a look of confusion followed by humor.

"What?"

"You're wearing my dressing gown," she remarked.

"You're wearing mine," he accused. "And it's rather arousing. Now, lie back and spread your legs apart."

Charlotte did the opposite, lifting her knees to her chest and wrapping her arms around them. Her gaze darted to the cloth he held. "What are you going to do?"

He gave her a quelling glance. "I'm going to wash you. The cool water should help lessen the sting."

Slowly unfolding her legs, Charlotte watched in wonder as he gently pressed the cloth to the insides of her thighs. "It doesn't hurt," she whispered, rather shocked at what he was doing—cleaning her in a manner even a lady's maid wouldn't do.

Moving back to the bowl of water, Adam rinsed the cloth and returned to the bed. "I apologize for being such a brute earlier," he said, continuing his ministrations. "I thought from the way Longburn strutted about town with you that he had bedded you rather regularly."

"And that bothered you?" she asked, inhaling softy when his touches with the cloth gentled and slowed.

"Immensely. Murder crossed my mind a few times, but it wouldn't have been very Christian of me," he murmured. He set the cloth aside. "Sit up for me," he said in a quiet voice.

Charlotte did as she was told. She helped him remove the banyan from her shoulders and arms and then gasped when he gripped the gathers of her night rail and lifted it from her body, tossing it over the side of the bed so it fluttered to the floor.

"Now, lie back," he murmured, pushing on her

shoulders. Charlotte complied, lowering her back to the bed. Before she realized he had moved down her body, he had his arms between her legs and his hands beneath the globes of her bottom and his head between her thighs.

The sudden sensation of his tongue on her most private place had Charlotte crying out in shock. Crying out from the sharp pang of pleasure that shot through her lower body. She inhaled, ready to put voice to a protest that was quickly replaced with another gasp as wave after wave of pleasure swept over her.

Her legs seemed as if they were no longer her own, her knees bent as they were, her thighs splayed wide as his tongue flicked over her womanhood.

As her mewls replaced the quiet, she thought of how she would look to anyone who walked in on them. Like a harlot, writhing in pleasure and in want of more. A hussy, freely offering her body and begging for whatever attentions she might attract.

The pleasure was that addictive. That powerful.

Charlotte was sure she could take no more of his ministrations when his tongue delved into her, and the pleasure changed into something far more consuming. Far more intense. For more pleasurable.

As her hands clutched the bed linens and her chest lifted from the bed, Charlotte cried out Adam's name.

Before she had even taken her next strangled breath, he was suddenly above her, over her, atop her, as his cock slipped into her in one, slow, torturous move.

She held her breath as he stilled, a mild curse sounding before his mouth covered one of her nipples. Lifting her knees to press against his thighs, she heard his curse turn into a prayer of thanks as his cock settled more deeply inside her.

Whatever his tongue had done to her womanhood, it was now doing to one hardened nipple, sending frissons of delight skittering beneath her skin before his mouth moved to the other and treated it to the same attentions.

With her head thrown back in the pillows, Charlotte watched through lowered lashes as Adam raised himself from her body, his arms holding him up as he pulled himself nearly all the way out of her body. She mewled a protest before he thrust into her, and then she watched as the cords of his neck stood out in relief. Another thrust and then another, and he stilled his movements as a wash of warmth filled her lower body.

Fearing he would pull his cock out of her, Charlotte clenched on it and moved her hands to the sides of his torso, hanging onto him as if her life depended on it.

Or perhaps his did, for he murmured words she didn't understand before he collapsed atop her.

This time, she didn't allow him to roll off of her, but held onto him by trapping his hips between her legs.

He might have chuckled or sobbed or swore—Charlotte couldn't make out what sounded from his throat—before he finally relaxed in her hold and fell asleep.

CHAPTER 30
LADY WILSON

A *few minutes later*

Charlotte stroked the fingers of her left hand through Adam's hair as he slept atop her, his head having ended up on her shoulder while the rest of his prone body covered hers in a heavy blanket of warmth.

His soft snores and even heartbeats against her breast were confirmations that he still lived, and although the weight of him made breathing harder for her, Charlotte didn't wish to be anywhere else. Even if Penelope chose that moment to come in search of her or for her father, Charlotte knew she would be hard pressed to react.

At some point, Adam had shed her dressing gown, and the thought of the girl finding her father naked had Charlotte feeling about with her other hand for the bed linens. She managed to pull them up and over most of his body, grinning when he mumbled something incoherent.

"Is it too soon to know that I feel affection for you?" he asked in a whisper.

Surprised by the query, Charlotte inhaled softly. "I should hope not," she replied, her voice sounding far away.

"Will you stay with me?"

Charlotte blinked awake. "Where would I go?"

She felt the vibrations of his chuckle through her entire body. "The mistress suite is next door," he whispered.

"If it's all the same, I'd like to stay right where I am."

Adam sighed, his chest relaxing once more onto hers. "Good. We'll give Harris the shock of his life in the morning when he comes with my coffee."

"Adam," she scolded.

"You've nothing to worry about. I've got you covered," he countered playfully.

"Barely." She inhaled, enjoying the scents of the citrus laundry soap and his cologne. Now more awake, the events of the evening came back to her in a flash. "You said something earlier about a proposal," she whispered.

"Hmph," Adam said as he dropped a kiss on her cheek and groaned. "I'll just be a moment."

Charlotte watched as he left the bed, his naked body illuminated by the single candle lamp. The golden angles and curves of his shoulders and back shifted as he moved, the muscles beneath his skin made more apparent by shadows. Despite the cool air in the bedchamber, his cock bobbed about in front of him, as if seeking her.

Swallowing, Charlotte sat up for a better vantage, shocked by how her own body responded as she gazed at him.

When he suddenly turned to regard her, he chuckled. "You've never seen a naked man before, have you?"

Charlotte swallowed again. "Only in statues at the British Museum," she replied, her voice breathy.

"Hmph." He turned so his backside was to her and opened a box on his dresser. "Not too disappointed, I hope?" he asked as his fingers rifled through the box.

"Oh, not at all," Charlotte replied as he made his way back to the bed. "You've a beautiful body."

"As do you," he whispered, his gaze darting down her torso and then back up again, somewhat disappointed that her breasts were hidden by her long red locks. "All that gorgeous hair." He glanced around the room. "I know I should probably be dressed appropriately to do this, but since you're naked, I rather like the idea of there being nothing between us," he explained as he lifted a hip and sat on the edge of the bed next to Charlotte. He was forced to close his eyes when one of her ripe nipples appeared between the strands of her hair.

He held out his hand, and upon the palm rested two rings. He lifted one between a thumb and forefinger and held it up. "This was my mother's. I'd like you to wear it on your left hand, as she did," he said as he slipped it onto her finger. He picked up the other. "This was Grandma Gertrude's," he said of the sapphire and diamond bauble. "I'd like you to wear it on your right hand," he said as he took her other hand and slipped the ring on her fourth finger.

"Two rings?" she asked in a whisper, holding out her hands side by side, the blue and red stones glimmering in the dim light of the candle lamp.

"Well, I could not decide," he replied with a shrug. "Will you marry me, Charlotte?"

She nodded before she wrapped her arms around his neck. "Yes. Yes, of course," she murmured, kissing his earlobe and his neck.

He wrapped an arm around her back and pulled her until she was sitting atop one of his thighs. Kissing the top of one of her breasts, he inhaled and let the breath out. "Well, that was rather anticlimactic," he murmured.

Attempting to suppress a giggle, Charlotte nearly shrieked when he nibbled on a pert nipple. "I cannot help but notice you're... you're aroused," she whispered. "Again."

He cleared his throat. "It's been a long time since I've bedded a woman, Charlotte," he admitted. "And you are naked."

"Then make love to me again," she whispered, her lips worrying his earlobe.

"You're going to be sore," he warned, even as he moved to stand. "As will I, I'm afraid," he added.

"I don't care if I am, Adam," she murmured, arching a brow as if she was daring him.

"Then I won't mind if I am, Lady Wilson," he said as he moved atop her.

He decided he didn't really mind a managing woman.

EPILOGUE

Two years later, the day after Easter, in the playroom of Wilson Hall

Her hands on her hips, Penelope stomped a slippered foot on the Turkish carpet and huffed. "Mother," she said in a plaintive voice.

"What is it, darling?" Charlotte asked as she looked up from the book she'd been reading aloud to Penelope and her brother, Winston. The boy was grinning ear to ear, his dark features resembling those of his father.

"He's knocked over our tower of blocks," she complained. "Again."

"Come here, you little ruffian," Charlotte said as she held out a hand to the toddler. He dutifully joined her at the settee and was attempting to climb onto it when she reached down and lifted him so he was sitting next to her. "You're vexing your sister, again."

The comment had the little boy even more amused, and a string of incomprehensible babbling ensued when he tipped over, his head ending up on her lap.

"Do you have any idea what he's saying?" Charlotte asked as she turned her attention on Penelope. The newly eight-year-old girl had changed her stance so her arms were crossed, a move that reminded Charlotte of what Adam would do when he was annoyed.

"How should I know?" she asked. "I haven't talked like that since I was that age."

"He's probably trying to let you know that it's time to leave for the village fair," Adam said as he made his way across the ballroom floor. "I know I'm ready to watch some juggling. And I've been asked to judge the baked goods," he added as he smacked his lips.

"Finally," Penelope said as her manner changed almost instantly. "I was beginning to think we weren't going."

"I had some business to finish up, Poppet," Adam remarked. He turned his attention on Charlotte. "Heard from Benjamin Turner of Turner Textiles in Reading. We're going to feature their silk in the shop," he said as he moved to the settee.

"Oh, that's wonderful, news" Charlotte replied,

knowing the addition of new silks in the London shop meant there would be fabrics available for her to have some gowns made for their trip to London the following month.

Adam lifted the boy into the air and then onto the crook of one arm, which sent Winston into a fit of giggles and more babbling.

"Come, let's go see what we can find at the village fair," he suggested as he held out an arm to Charlotte. "I hear there's going to be a wedding on the stage following the sword swallower."

Penelope's eyes widened. "Who's getting married?" she asked in awe.

"Our very own housekeeper," Charlotte replied.

"And our groom will be the groom, although now that Mr. Smithton has agreed to take on managing the tenant cottages, Mr. Coulsden will be our driver, and he will manage the stable."

"I'm so glad he has accepted the position," Charlotte remarked as she held out a hand for Penelope.

"So is Mrs. McNulty," Adam replied as they made their way down the stairs. "Apparently, my cousin didn't think she would have anything to do with a mere groom."

"But... she would have wed him two years ago if he'd asked," Charlotte said.

Adam decided not to mention that William Coulsden had indeed asked Margaret McNulty to marry him the same night he had proposed to Charlotte. Decided not to mention that Mrs. McNulty had agreed to William's proposal. That the two of them had already been behaving as if they were a married couple. Adam had given the housekeeper permission to use the guest bedroom as her quarters before Charlotte and he had said their vows, and he knew the groom was sharing the room with her.

"Well, it's not as if they had to be concerned about starting a family, given their ages," Adam said, chuckling when Winston started another round of babbles, one of his fingers waving in the direction of Charlotte.

"I guess this means he wants to sit next to you," Adam said.

"He's certainly been doing so more of late," Charlotte remarked as she pulled on her Merino wool redingote. She helped Penelope into her matching coat as Adam saw to the boy.

Once in the coach, Adam sat next to Penelope, and Winston crawled up next to Charlotte. When the coach rumbled off toward Cockington, Winston turned around in his seat and placed his head on Charlotte's lap, facing her.

"What *are* you doing?" she asked before he patted her middle and once again started babbling.

Penelope crossed her arms and let out a huff. "Can't you see? He's talking to the baby, of course," she said. "And it had better be a girl this time."

Adam blinked as he turned his attention on his wife. "Baby?" he repeated. "What baby?"

Charlotte's mouth dropped open before she glanced down at the boy and then gave her husband a guilty shrug. "I was going to tell you later this evening," she claimed. "I'm with child." Her gaze fell on Winston. "But... how did *you* know, little man?"

Winston continued happily babbling as Adam moved to her side of the coach and sat next to her. He kissed her quite thoroughly as Penelope rolled her eyes and sighed in defeat.

AUTHOR NOTES

Cardboard Cartons

The first cardboard boxes were made in England in 1817.

News-sheets

The *Torquay Chronicle* is purely fictitious. Although there were dozens of news-sheets published in Devonshire when this story takes place, the two main publications were the *Western Times* and the *Exeter Flying Post*, both printed in Exeter.

ABOUT THE AUTHOR

A self-described nerd and student of history, Linda Rae spent many years as a published technical writer specializing in 3D graphics workstations, software and 3D animation (her movie credits include SHREK and SHREK 2). Getting lost in the rabbit holes of research has resulted in historical romances set in the Regency-era as well as Ancient Greece.

A fan of action-adventure movies, she can frequently be found at the local cinema. Although she no longer has any tropical fish, she follows the San Jose Sharks and makes her home in Cody, Wyoming.

For more information:
www.lindaraesande.com
Sign up for Linda Rae's newsletter:
Regency Romance with a Twist
Follow Linda Rae's blog:
Regency Romance with a Twist